AMERICAN MORONS

STORIES BY
Glen Hirshberg

AMERICAN MORONS

STORIES BY
Glen Hirshberg

Earthling Publications 2006

First edition, first printing
October 2006

ISBN (trade hardcover): 0-9766339-8-1

Previous versions of these stories originally appeared in the following publications:
"American Morons" in *Darkness Rising: The Rolling Darkness Revue Chapbook 2005*.
"Like a Lily in a Flood" in *Cemetery Dance* #50, 2004.
"Flowers on Their Bridles, Hooves in the Air" on Scifiction.com, 2003.
"Safety Clowns" in *Acquainted with the Night*, Ash-Tree Press, 2004.
"Transitway" in *Cemetery Dance* #56, 2006.

"Devil's Smile" and "The Muldoon" are original to this collection.

A signed limited edition of this book has also been published; please contact Earthling Publications for details.

EARTHLING PUBLICATIONS
P.O. Box 413
Northborough, MA 01532 USA
Website: www.earthlingpub.com
Email: earthlingpub@yahoo.com

Printed in the U.S.A.

For John, who somehow figured out that
almost all of it is funny, and then taught me that.

And for Kim, and Sid, and Kate,
with shipwrecks and merry-go-rounds and ice-cream trucks
and my grandfather, whom I wish you'd known.

Contents

American Morons

"Omnibus umbra locis adero: dabis, improbe, poenas."

("My angry ghost, arising from the deep
Shall haunt thee waking, and disturb thy sleep.")
—Virgil

In the end, the car made it more than a mile after leaving the gas station, all the way to the tollgate that marked the outskirts of Rome. Ignoring the horns behind them and the ominous, hacking rattle of the engine, the two Americans dug together through the coins they'd dumped in the dashboard ashtray. Twice, Kellen felt Jamie's sweat-streaked fingers brush his. The horn blasts got more insistent, and Jamie laughed, so Kellen did, too.

When they'd finally assembled the correct change, he threw the coins into the bin, where they clattered to the bottom except for one ten-cent piece that seemed to stick in the mesh. Ruefully, Kellen imagined turning, trying to motion everyone behind him back so he could reverse far enough out of the toll island to open his door and climb out. Then the coin dropped and disappeared into the bottom of the basket.

Green light flashed. The gate rose. Kellen punched the accelerator and felt it plunge straight down. There was not even a rattle, now.

"Uh, Kel?" Jamie said.

As though they'd heard her, or could see his foot on the dead edal, every car in the queue let loose with an all-out sonic barrage.

Then—since this was Italy, where blasting horns at fellow drivers was like showering rice on newlyweds—most of the cars in the queues to either side joined in.

Expressionlessly, Kellen turned in his seat, his skin unsticking from the rental's cracked, roasted vinyl with a pop. The setting sun blazed through the windshield into his eyes. "At least," he said, "it's not like you warned me the car might only take diesel."

"Yes I—"Jamie started, caught the irony, and stopped. She'd been in the midst of retying her maple syrup hair on the back of her neck. Kellen found himself watching her tank top spaghetti strap slide in the slickness on her shoulder as she spoke again. "At least it doesn't say the word *DIESEL* in big green letters on the gas cap."

He looked up, blinking. "Does it really?"

"Saw it lying on the trunk while that attendant dude was trying whatever he was trying to fix it. What'd he pour in there, anyway?"

Goddamnit, Kellen snarled inside his own head for perhaps the thousandth time in the past week. Jamie and he had been a couple all the way through high school. Three years into their separate college lives, he still considered them one. She said she did, too. *And she wasn't lying, exactly.* But he'd felt the change all summer long. He'd thought this trip might save them.

A particularly vicious horn blast from the car behind almost dislodged his gaze. Almost. "At least *diesel* isn't the same word in Italian as it is in English," he said, and Jamie burst out laughing.

"Time to meet more friendly Romans."

Too late, Kellen started issuing his by now familiar warning, cobbled from their parents' pre-trip admonishments about European attitudes toward Americans at the moment, plus the words that had swirled around them all week, blaring from radios, the front pages of newspapers they couldn't read, TV sets in the lobbies of youth hostels they'd stayed in just for the adventure, since their respective parents had supplied plenty of hotel money. *Cadavere. Sesto Americano. George Bush. Pavone.* Not that

Jamie would have listened, anyway. He watched her prop her door open and stick out one tanned, denim-skirted leg.

Instantly, the horns shut off. Doors in every direction popped like champagne corks, and within seconds, half a dozen Italian men of wildly variant ages and decisions about chest hair display fizzed around the Americans' car.

"Stuck," Jamie said through her rolled down window. "Um. *Kaput.*"

"I'm pretty sure that's not Ital—" Kellen started, but before he could finish, his door was ripped open. Startled, he twisted in his seat. The man pouring himself into the car wore no shirt whatsoever, and was already gripping the wheel. The rest of the men fanned into formation, and then the car was half-floating, half-rolling through the tollgate into traffic that made no move to slow, but honked gleefully as it funneled around them. Seconds later, they glided to a stop on the gravel shoulder.

Jamie leaned back in her seat, folding her arms and making a great show of sighing like a queen in a palanquin. Whether her grin was for him or the guy who'd grabbed the steering wheel, Kellen had no idea. The guy hadn't let go, and Kellen remained pinned in place.

What was it about Italian men that made him want to sprout horns and butt something? "I say again," he murmured to Jamie. "*Kaput?*"

"It's one of those universal words, ol' pal. Like 'diesel'." Then she was lifted out of the car.

Even Jamie seemed taken aback, and made a sort of chirping sound as the throng enveloped her. "*Bella,*" Kellen heard one guy coo, and something that sounded like "*Assistere,*" and some tongue-clucking that could have been regret over the car or wolfish slavering over Jamie or neither. Kellen didn't like that he could no longer see her, and he didn't like the forearm stretched across his chest.

Abruptly, it lifted, and he wriggled out fast and stood. The man before him looked maybe forty, with black and gray curly hair, a muscular chest, and Euro-sandals with those straps that pulled the big toes too far from their companions. He said nothing to Kellen, and instead watched Jamie slide sunglasses over her eyes, whirling amid her circle of admirers with her skirt lifting above her knee every time she turned. Back home, Jamie was borderline pretty—slim, athletic, a little horse-faced—at least until she laughed. But in Italy, judging from the response of the entire male population during their week in Rome and Tuscany, she was a Goddess. Or else all women were.

Ol' pal. That's what he was, now.

Almost seven o'clock, and still the blazing summer heat poured down. Two more miles, Kellen thought, and he and Jamie could at least have stood in one of Rome's freezing fountains while they waited for the tow truck. Jamie would have left her loafers on the pavement, her feet bare.

"It's okay, thanks guys," he said abruptly, and started around the car. Digging into his shorts pocket for his cell phone, he waved it at the group like a wand that might make them disappear. "*Grazie.*" His accent sounded pathetic, even to him.

Not a single Italian turned. One of them, he noticed, had his hand low on Jamie's back, and another had stepped in close alongside, and Kellen stopped feeling like butting anything and got nervous. And more sad.

"All set, guys. Thanks a lot." His hand was in his pocket again, lifting out his wallet and opening it to withdraw a fistful of five-Euro notes. Jamie glanced at him, and her mouth turned down hard as her eyes narrowed. The guy with the sandals made that clucking sound again and stepped up right behind Kellen.

For a second, Kellen went on waving the money, knowing he shouldn't, not sure why he felt like such an asshole. Only after he stopped moving did he realize no one but Jamie was looking at him.

In fact, no one was anywhere near them anymore. All together, the men who'd encircled Jamie and the sandal guy were retreating toward the tollgate. Catching Kellen's glance, sandal guy lifted one long, hairy arm. *Was that a wave?*

Then they were alone. Just he, Jamie, the cars revving pas

each other as they reentered the laneless *superstrade*, and the other car, parked maybe fifty feet ahead of them. Yellow, encased in grit, distinctly European-box. The windows were so grimy that Kellen couldn't tell whether anyone was in there. But someone had to be, because the single sharp honk that had apparently scattered their rescuers had come from there.

"What was that bullshit with the money?" Jamie snapped. "They're not waiters. They were help—"

The scream silenced her. Audible even above the traffic, it soared over the retaining wall beyond the shoulder and seemed to unfurl in the air before dissipating. In the first instant, Kellen mistook it for a siren.

Glancing at Jamie, then the retaining wall, then the sun squatting on the horizon, he stepped closer. He felt panicky, for all sorts of reasons. He also didn't want this trip to end, ever. "Got another one of those universal words for you, James. Been in the papers all week. Ready? *Cadaver.*"

"*Cadavere,*" Jamie said, her head twisted around toward the origin of the scream.

"Right."

Together, they collapsed into leaning positions against their rented two-seater. It had been filthy when they got it—cleanliness apparently not the business necessity here that it was back home—and now sported a crust as thick as Tuscan bread.

"Well, you got that thing out." She was gesturing at the cell phone in his hands, and still sounded pissed. "Might as well use it."

Kellen held it up, feeling profoundly stupid. "Forgot to charge."

Instantly, Jamie was smiling again, bending forward to kiss him on the forehead, which was where she always kissed him these days.

"Sorry about the money thing," Kellen said, clinging to her smile. "I didn't mean anything bad, I was just..."

"Establishing dominance. Very George Bush."

"Dominance? I was about as dominant as...I was being nice.

I was showing appreciation. Sincere appreciation. If not for those guys, we'd still be—"

The passenger door of the yellow car swung open, and Kellen stopped talking.

His first thought, as the guy unfolded onto the gravel, was that he shouldn't have been able to fit in there. This was easily the tallest Italian Kellen had seen all week. And the thinnest, and lightest-skinned. The hair on his head shone lustrous and long and black. For a few seconds, he stood swaying with his back to them, like some roadside reed that had sprung up from nowhere. Then he turned.

Just a boy, really. Silvery blue eyes that sparkled even from fifteen feet away, and long-fingered hands that spread over his bare, spindly legs like stick-bugs clinging to a branch. The driver's side door opened, and a second figure tumbled out.

This one was a virtual opposite of his companion, short and stumpy, with curly, dirty hair that bounced on the shoulders of his striped red rugby shirt. He wore red laceless canvas shoes. Black stubble stuck out of his cheeks like porcupine quills and all but obscured his goofy, ear-to-ear smile. He stopped one step behind the reedy kid. All Kellen could think of was *prince* and *troll.*

"*Ciao,*" said the troll, his smile somehow broadening as he bounded forward. Unlike everyone else they'd met here, he looked at Kellen at least as much Jamie. "*Ciao.*" He ran both hands over the hood of the rental car, then seemed to hold his breath, as though checking for a heartbeat.

"*Parla Inglese?*" Jamie tried.

"*Americano?*"

"Ye—" Kellen started, and Jamie overrode him.

"Canadian."

"*Si. Americano.*" Bouncing up and down on his heels, the troll grinned his prickly grin. "George Bush. Bang bang."

"John Kerry," Jamie said, rummaging in her purse and pulling out one of the campaign buttons her mother had demanded she keep there, as though it were mace. She waved i at the troll, who merely raised his bushy eyebrows and stared a question at them.

"What?" Kellen said. *"Non parlo L'Italiano."*

"He didn't say anything, idiot," Jamie said, then gasped and stumbled forward.

Whirling, Kellen found the reedy boy directly behind them, staring down. He really was tall. And his eyes were deep-water blue. *Nothing frightening about him,* Kellen thought, wondering why his heart was juddering like that.

"Mi dispiace." This one's voice rang, sonorous and way too big for its frame, like a bell-peal. From over the retaining wall, another one of those screams bloomed in the air, followed by a second and third in rapid succession.

"Howler monkeys?" Kellen said softly to Jamie. "What the hell is that?"

But Jamie was casting her eyes back and forth between the two Italians. The troll pointed at the hood of their car, then raised his hands again.

"Oh," Jamie said. "The gas. My friend put in…"

The troll cocked his head and smiled uncomprehendingly.

Abruptly, Jamie started around to the gas tank and came back with the cap. She pointed it toward the troll. "See? Diesel."

"Diesel. *Si.*"

"No diesel." Forming her fingers into a sort of gun, Jamie mimed putting a pump into the tank. "Gas."

For one more moment, the troll just stood. Then his hands flew to his cheeks. "Ohhh. Gas. No diesel. Ohhh." Still grinning, he drew one of his fingers slowly across his own throat. Then he let loose a stream of Italian.

After a minute or so of that, Kellen held up his cell phone. "You have one?" He was trying to control his embarrassment. And his ridiculous unease.

"Ohhh," the troll said, glancing at his companion.

Reedy boy's smile was regal and slow. He said nothing at all.

"Ohhh." Now, the troll seemed to be dancing as he moved 'round the front of the car. Instinctively, Kellen stepped a half pace back toward the retaining wall, just to feel a little less like he and Jamie were being maneuvered in between these two. "In America, auto break, call. Someone come." He snapped his fingers. "But *a l'Italia*...ohhh." He smacked his palm to his forehead and made a Jerry Lewis grimace.

The troll's grunting laugh—unlike reedy boy's voice—simply annoyed Kellen. "They'll come. You have?" He waved the cell phone again.

"Why are you talking like that?" Jamie snapped.

"You have one? This one's..." He waved the phone some more, looking helplessly at his girlfriend. *Friend*, she'd said. "*Kaput.*"

"Ah!" said prickly guy. "*Si. Si.*" With another glance toward his companion, he raced back to the yellow car and stuck his head and hands inside the window. From the way his body worked, he was still yammering and gesturing as he rummaged around in there. Then he was back, waving a slim, black phone. He flipped open the faceplate, put it to his ears, then raised the other hand in the questioning gesture again.

"I'll do it," Kellen said, reached out, and reedy boy seemed to lean forward. But he made no blocking movement as his companion handed over the phone.

"Thanks. *Grazie*," Kellen said, while Jamie beamed her brightest naïve, Kerry-loving smile at both Italians. Kellen's father said all Kerry supporters smiled like that. Jamie was quite possibly the only Democrat Kellen's father loved.

He had his fingers on the keypad before he realized the problem. "Shit," he barked.

The troll grinned. "Ohhh."

"What?" Jamie asked, stepping nearer. "Just call someone. Call American Express."

"You know the number?"

"I thought you did."

"It's on speed dial on my phone. My dad programmed it in. I've never even looked at it."

"Get your card."

"They didn't give me that card. They gave me the Visa."

"*Mi scusi*," said the troll, stepping close as yet another of those long, shrieking cries erupted from behind the retaining wall. Reedy boy just looked briefly over his shoulder at the yellow car before returning his attention to Jamie and Kellen. Neither of the Italians seemed even to have heard the screams.

Tapping his red-striped chest, the troll reached out and chattered more Italian. Kellen had no idea what he was saying, but handed him the phone. Nodding, the troll punched in numbers. For a good minute, he stood with the phone at his ear, grinning. Then he started speaking fast into the mouthpiece, turning away and walking off down the shoulder.

"We're pretty lucky these guys are here to help," Jamie said against his ear.

Kellen glanced at her. She had her arms tucked in tight to her chest, her bottom lip curled against her teeth. For the first time, he realized she might be even more on edge than he was. She'd seen the same stories he had, after all. Same photos. The couple left dangling upside down from a flagpole outside the Colosseum, tarred and feathered and wrapped in the Stars and Stripes. The whole Tennessee family discovered laid out on a Coca-Cola blanket inside the ruins of a recently excavated two thousand-year-old catacomb near the Forum, all of them naked, gutted from genitalia to xiphoid, stuffed with feathers. The couple on the flagpole had reminded Jamie of a paper she'd written on Ancient Rome, something about a festival where puppets got hung in trees. The puppets took the place of the little boys once sacrificed on whatever holiday that was.

The troll had walked all the way back to his yellow car, now, and he was talking animatedly, waving his free arm around and sometimes holding the cell phone in front of his face and shouting into it. Reedy boy simply stood, still as a sentry, gazing placidly over Kellen and Jamie's heads toward the tollgate.

Overhead, the sun sank toward the retaining wall, and the air didn't cool, exactly, but thinned. Despite the unending honks and tire squeals from the A1, Kellen found something almost soothing about the traffic. There was a cheerfulness to it that rendered it completely different from the American variety. The horns reminded him mostly of squawking birds.

On impulse, he slid his arm around Jamie's shoulders. Her skin felt hot but dry. Her flip-flopped foot tapped in the dirt. She neither leaned into him nor away. Years from now, he knew, they'd be telling this story. To their respective children, not the children he'd always thought they'd have together. As an excuse to tell it, just once more, to each other.

At least, that's how it would be for him. "Diesel," he muttered. "Who uses diesel anymore?"

"People who care about the air. Diesel's a million times cleaner than regular gas."

"But it stinks."

She shook off his arms.

"You smell anything?"

Kellen realized that he didn't.

"They fixed the smell problem ages ago. You're just brainwashed."

"Brainwashed?"

"Oil company puppet. George Bush puppet. Say W, little puppet."

"W," said Kellen, tried a smile though he still felt unsettled and dumb, and Jamie smiled weakly back, without taking her eyes off the placid face of the thin boy.

"Okay!" called the troll, waving. He stuck his head into the yellow car, continuing to gesture even though no one could see him, then reemerged. "*Arrivo. Si?* Coming."

Jamie smiled her thanks. Reedy boy turned his head enough to watch the sun as it vanished. Shadows poured over the retaining wall onto the freeway, and with them came a chorus of shrieks that flooded the air and took a long time evaporating.

Squeezing Jamie once on the elbow in what he hoped was a reassuring manner, Kellen made his way around their dead rental, climbed the dirt incline that rimmed the *superstrade*, and reached the retaining wall, which was taller than it looked. Ever standing at its base, Kellen couldn't see over the top. The wall was made of the same chipped, ancient-looking stone that dotted excavation sites all over Italy. What, Kellen wondered, had this originally been built to retain?

Standing on tiptoe, he dropped his elbows on top of the stone, wedged a foot into the grit between rocks, and hoisted himself up. There he hung, elbows grinding into the wall, mouth wide open.

Without letting go, he turned his head after a few seconds. "Jamie," he said quietly, hoping somehow to attract her and not the reedy boy. But his voice didn't carry over the traffic, and Jamie didn't turn around. Against the yellow car, the troll leaned, smoking a thin, brownish cigarette. "*Jamie*," Kellen barked, and she glanced up, and the reedy boy, too, slowly. "Jamie, come here."

She came. Right as she reached the base of the wall, the screeching started once more. Knowing the source, as he now did, should have reassured Kellen. Instead, he closed his eyes and clutched the stone.

"Kel?" Jamie said, her voice so small, suddenly, that Kellen could barely hear it. "Kellen, what's up there?"

He opened his eyes, staring over the wall again. "Peacock Auschwitz."

"Will you stop saying shit like that? You sound like your stupid president, except he probably thinks Auschwitz is a beer."

"He's your president, too."

She was struggling to get her feet wedged into the chinks in the wall. He could have helped, or told her to stay where she was, but did neither.

"Oh, God," she said, as soon as she'd climbed up beside him. Then she went silent, too.

The neighborhood looked more like a gypsy camp than a slum. The tiny, collapsing houses seemed less decayed than pieced together out of discarded tires, chicken wire, and old stones. The shadows streaming over everything now had already pooled down there, so that the olive trees scattered everywhere looked like hunched old people, white-haired, slouching through the ruins like mourners in a graveyard.

Attached to every single structure—even the ones where roofs had caved in, walls given way—was a cage, as tall as the houses, lined with some kind of razor wire with the sharp points twisted inward. Inside the cages were birds.

Peacocks. Three, maybe four to a house, including the ones that were already dead. The live ones paced skittishly, great tails dragging in the dust, through the spilled innards and chopped bird feet lining the cage bottoms. There was no mistaking any of it, and even if there were, the reek that rose from down there was a clincher. Shit and death. Unmistakable.

In the cage nearest them, right at the bottom of the wall, one bird glanced up, lifted its tail as though considering throwing it open, then tilted its head back and screamed.

"You know," said the reedy boy, right beneath them, in perfect though faintly accented English, and Kellen and Jamie jerked. Then they just hung, clinging to the wall. "The Ancient Romans sacrificed the *pavone*—the peacock, *si?*—to honor their emperors. They symbolized immortality. And their tails were the thousand eyes of God, watching over our civilization. Of course, they also sacrificed humans, to the *Larvae*."

Very slowly, still clutching the top of the wall, Kellen turned his head. The boy was so close that Kellen could feel the exhalation of his breath on the sweat still streaming down his back. Even if Kellen had tried a kick, he wouldn't have been able to get anything on it. Jamie had gone rigid, and when he glanced that way, he saw that her eyes had teared up, though they remained fixed unblinkingly on the birds below.

"Larvae?" he asked, just to be talking. He couldn't think what else to do. "Like worms?"

"Dead men. Demons, really. Demons made of dead, bad men."

"Why?"

"Yes!" The boy nodded enthusiastically, folding his hands in that contemplative, regal way. "You are right. To invoke the

Larvae and set them upon the enemies of Rome? Or to pacify them, and in doing so drive away ill fortune? Which is the correct course? I would guess even they did not always know. What is your guess?"

That I'm about to die, Kellen thought crazily, closed his eyes, and bit his lip to keep from crying out like the peacocks beneath him. "So Romans cherished their dead, bad men?"

"And their sacrifices. And their executioners. Like all human civilizations do."

Carefully, expecting a dagger to his ribs at any moment, Kellen eased his elbows off the stone, let one leg drop, then the other. The birds had gone silent. He stood a second, face to the stone. Then he turned.

The reedy boy was fifteen feet away, head aimed down the road as he walked slowly to his car.

"Jamie," Kellen hissed, and Jamie skidded down the wall to land next to him.

"Ow," she murmured, crooking her elbow to reveal an ugly red scrape.

"Jamie. Are we in trouble?"

She looked at him. He'd never seen the expression on her face before. But he recognized it instantly, and it chilled him almost as much as the reedy boy's murmur. *Contempt.* He'd always been terrified she'd show him that, sooner or later. And also certain that someday she would.

Without a word, she walked down the dirt incline, holding her elbow against her chest. When she reached the car, she stuck out a forefinger and began trailing it through the dirt on the driver's side window.

Okay, Kellen urged himself. *Think.* They had no phone. And who would they call? What was 911 in Italian? Maybe they could just walk fast toward the tollgate. Run out in traffic. People would honk. But they'd also see them. Nothing could happen as long as someone was looking, right?

Then he remembered the way the men who'd helped them to the shoulder had vanished. His mind veered into a skid.

They all know. The whole country. An agreement they've come to. They knew the yellow car, the location. The birds. They knew. They left us here. Put us here. Even the guy at the gas station, just what had he poured in the tank to supposedly save them?

Peacock screams. A whole chorus of them, as the last light went out of the day. Kellen scrambled fast down the dirt toward the car, toward Jamie, who was crouched on the gravel now, head down and shaking back and forth on her long, tanned neck.

At the same moment, he saw both what Jamie had scrawled in the window grime and the two men by the yellow car starting toward them again. They came side by side, the reedy boy with one long-fingered hand on the stumpy one's shoulders.

AMERICAN MORONS. That's what she'd written.

"I love you," Kellen blurted. She didn't even look up.

The men from the yellow car were twenty feet away, now, ignoring the cars, the bird-screams, everything but their quarry.

Hop the wall, Kellen thought. But the idea of hiding in that neighborhood—of just setting foot in it—seemed even worse than facing down these two. Also, weirdly, like sacrilege. *Like parading with camera bags and iPods and cell phones through places where people had prayed, played with, and killed each other.*

This was what he was thinking, as the two Romans ambled ever nearer, when the truck loomed up, let loose a gloriously throaty, brain-clearing honk, and settled with a sigh right beside them.

"We're saved," he whispered, then dropped to his knees as the first and only girl he'd loved finally looked up. "Jamie, the tow truck's here. We're saved."

In no time at all, the driver was out, surveying the ruined rental, shoving pieces of puffy, cold pizza into their hands. He didn't speak English either, just gestured with emphatic Italian clarity. The cab of his truck was for him and his pizza. Jamie and Kellen could ride in their car. They climbed back in, and as the driver attached a chain and winch to the bumper, began to drag them onto the long, high bed of the truck, Kellen thought about blasting his horn, giving a chin-flick to the yellow-car guys.

Except that that was ridiculous. The yellow-car guys had called the tow truck. There'd never been any danger at all.

He started to laugh, put his hand on Jamie's. She was shivering, though it was still a long way from cold. The tow truck driver chained them into place, climbed back into his cab. Only then did it occur to Kellen that now they were really trapped.

With a lurch, the truck edged two wheels onto the *super-strade*, answering a volley of horn blares with a bazooka blast of its own. Perched there, eight feet off the ground, chained in the car on the tow truck bed, Kellen had a perfect view of the blue Mercedes coupe as it swerved onto the shoulder directly behind the yellow car. He saw the driver climb out of the blue car, wearing a black poncho that made no sense in the heat.

Stepping away from his own door, this new arrival simply watched as the reedy guy pointed a command and the troll dragged a little boy, bound in rusty wire, kicking and hurling his gagged head from side to side, out of the back seat of the yellow car. All too clearly, Kellen saw the boy's face. So distinctly American he could practically picture it on a milk carton already. Wheat-blond hair, freckles like crayon dots all over his cheeks, Yankees cap still somehow wedged over his ears.

Except it would never wind up on a milk carton, Kellen realized, grabbing at the useless steering wheel. *When he'd called home to tell his father about the murders, his father had snorted and said, "Thus proving there are ungrateful malcontents in Italy just like here." No one else they'd called had even heard the news. This boy would simply evaporate into the new American history, like the dead soldiers lined up in their coffins in that smuggled photograph from the second Gulf War.*

Shuddering himself now, still holding the wheel, Kellen wondered where the boy's face would appear in its Italian newspaper photo. *Drowned in a fountain atop the Spanish Steps? Wedged into one of the slits in the underground walls of Nero's Cryptoporticus? Strewn amid the refuse and scraps of fast-food wrappers and discarded homeless-person shoes along the banks of the Tiber?*

Just as the truck rumbled forward, plowing a space for itself in the traffic, the guy in the poncho closed the door of his Mercedes on his new passenger, and both the troll and the reedy boy looked up and caught Kellen's eyes.

The troll waved. The reedy boy smiled.

Like a Lily in a Flood

"White and golden Lizzie stood,
Like a lily in a flood;
Like a rock of blue-vein'd stone
Lash'd by tides obstreperously;
Like a beacon left alone
In a hoary roaring sea..."
                                    —Christina Rossetti

"Tho*reau*?" his hostess snorts, setting down the small china plate of molasses cookies wrapped in linen at his elbow. Where he sits on the veranda, the evening is already cool—amazing, given the stifling heat of the day—and he can feel the warmth from the cookies on the skin of his arm like a hot water bottle. "I'll give you your Thoreau." His hostess straightens, long and swanlike in her white summer sweater. Her hair is undyed, white and simple, cut short.

Closing his book on his finger, Nagle leans back against the wicker, happy to be here. Happier than he will admit to Melinda when he gets home tomorrow night. Probably, next time, he should bring her. His hostess would like her more than he suspects she liked Elise, because Melinda is tougher. He watches the boughs of the red cedars rustle along the curving bank of Lake Waukewan as the bats and evening grosbeaks stir to meet the moon.

"All right," he says. "Give me my Thoreau."

"My great-great-great grandmother Mary used to trudge all the way out there twice a week, more than six miles each way, to fetch his washing and return it to him. That's your back-to-nature, live-pure, transcend-yourself Thoreau."

Nagle expects her to tromp back inside—she has always been fond of exit lines—but instead she folds her arms and stands beside his chair, eyes clear blue, spine stiff and straight as the trunk of a spruce pine.

"Now I know," he says.

For a few moments, they stay together on the veranda while loon call erupts over the lake. Out front, a mobile home blunders down the access road toward the campground a mile or so away. Two thoughts occur to Nagle simultaneously: first, that he has been coming here for over twenty-three years, ever since he had the urge to see where his parents had stayed on the night before their death, and in all that time, he has never seen his hostess stand still this long; and second, never before has he been here when none of the other three guest rooms have been occupied. In fact, he can't remember *any* of the other rooms ever being vacant.

His hostess unfolds her arms and slaps her palms against her blue-jeaned thighs. "Come inside, I'll find you something a mite *fresher* to read." She starts for the doorway. "Come soon. Mosquitoes fit to suck your eyes out this year." She waves her arm in the air, and a trail of midges seems to float off her fingers as though she has conjured them.

"Mosquitoes don't bother with me, much," he says, as she bangs back through the screen door, which slaps into place behind her.

This is the first time she has offered him a literary recommendation. He will wait, he thinks, just long enough to provide the appearance of disinterest both he and his hostess are most comfortable with.

So for ten minutes, he sits. He loves the lake at twilight, the motorboats and Jet Skis returning to their berths, the loons circling as tiny black waterbugs skitter over the surface of the water like the crowd at the end of a high school football game, the light almost standoffish, flat greens and golds, nothing flashy like the sunsets over the ocean or even a polluted city. Elise had loved this, too. Melinda would want to go find the nearest Putt-Putt, then get a beer. She would have her kinked hair corded, and she'd be well into the third of her three-every-evening smokes, singing Patsy Cline. What is it that keeps him from bringing her here? Maybe it's simply the nature of their relationship, which is also the nature, he is willing to bet, of most serious second relationships with both partners over forty and no kids involved: he and Melinda get on well, and they each leave the things the other loves alone.

He stands and passes quietly through the screen door into the den with its comfortably stuffed but fraying white couches, its framed photographs he assumes were taken by his hostess: a black bear rising on two legs beside the white ash off the veranda; the Frozen Joy ice cream shack over in New Sandwich, its lot uncharacteristically empty of Winnebagos; one of those tiny roadside New Hampshire cemeteries that house at least one dead soldier from the Revolutionary War and three or four infants, with tree roots enfolding their graves like mothers' arms. He is halfway through the dining room when he realizes it isn't just the absence of other guests that has made the house seem bare. It's that none of the four round breakfast tables in the dining room have been set with so much as a water glass.

Maybe, he thinks, his hostess no longer considers him a guest. But he knows right away that's ridiculous. So maybe something terrible has happened, someone has died or moved away. At the moment, he does not want to ask. He hasn't even asked Melinda that sort of question, and he has appreciated not being asked himself.

Before habit set in, it was the square, red-carpeted library tucked right off the kitchen that lured him back here those first few summers—the mushy yellow recliners, fire lit on cool nights, lamps filled with paraffin and the electric lights switched off. Not for the first time, standing in this room, he wonders what it would be like to have books as his workday tools, rather than circular saws and levels and four-by-fours. But the jobs that involve reading also require more engagement with people than he generally enjoys, and of course he might not love reading so much if he had to do it for a living, and if everyone around him was reading, too.

Here, books are crammed every which way on the sturdy maple shelves. The verticals are lacquered walnut straight up to the ceiling. Skirting the recliners, Nagle peruses the collection, impressed, as he is every year, by its variety, by its almost willful *oddness*, as though each succeeding owner of this home had her own monomania and pursued it relentlessly.

He starts in the northwest corner, with the four complete rows of New Hampshire-set murder mysteries. There is one, it seems, for every lake and notable site in the state, such as *Murder on the Mount*. Climbing the library ladder, he lingers momentarily at the shelf full of nasty-looking proper parenting books from the 1920s and '30s with vaguely ominous titles like *When Your Child is Bad*. Never once has he pulled down one of these books, though they have always intrigued him, strangely. So have the books on the row above them about making ham radios, with their bright blue and red spines cracked from overuse, their titles—*You Can Tune in the Moon* is his particular favorite—a cheerful mirror to the parenting volumes. Clambering up even farther to his favorite shelves, jammed with disordered, leather-bound editions of the classics, Nagle reaches for a slim, gray volume whose title he does not recognize, then stops and stares at the shelf. Surely, he thinks, it's a trick of the lamplight.

But it's no trick. All these years he has been pulling books off the wall and somehow he has never noticed the long, rectangular panel cut into the back of this bookcase. He wouldn't have noticed it tonight, except that whoever slid the door open last had closed it clumsily, leaving it slightly off kilter, not quite shut.

Nagle pops the panel back into place and slides it open, then glances around fast, suddenly aware that his hostess might perceive this as snooping. She is nowhere to be seen. He should shut the door. Instead, he listens. He hears an owl, a dog, crickets, then loon call echoing over the water, not ghostly, just wild, a sound our throats simply cannot make. He hears his own breath, the ladder creaking beneath his weight. It has been so long since he has felt himself near the secret center of anything.

He slides a hand into the space he has uncovered. For a second, he believes there is nothing, and then his fingers brush leather, and he pulls out three dusty, chipped leather hardbacks, washed-out green and lashed together with twine. The books feel light in his hands, the leather too soft, like embalmed skin. The covers are blank, and he finds only dates on the spines. *1840—. 1850—. 1870—.* He sets them down carefully on the ladder's top step.

Reaching through the opening again, Nagle pads around once more and withdraws another set of books. The top volume is black and says *C. Rossetti Poems* in faded gilt lettering along the spine. The other is blue and badly foxed. The spine says, *Holy Bible.*

"Ah," says his hostess from the doorway, which startles him so badly that he nearly tips the set of dated volumes off the ladder and himself along with them.

Blushing, holding his breath, Nagle waits. The feeling is considerably worse than—and really nothing like—being caught stealing from his uncle's wallet at the age of twelve, a few years after his parents' accident in the White Mountains, less than thirty miles from here. They'd been riding the sky-tram up a steep mountainside when the cables snapped and plunged their car—with the two of them in it, holding each other—two hundred feet into the gorge below. The cable company had furiously denied negligence in maintaining the tram, but the out-of-court settlement had bought his uncle's house and paid for Nagle's three years of college before he dropped out. Small compensation.

"I'm…sorry," he finally stammers, "I was just—"

"Better watch the scorpions," she says, gazing at him steadily. Her eyes are actually more gray than blue. Frozen lakewater. "Book-scorpions. Nasty little spiders that rest in old bindings. I've got the bites to prove it." She lifts one hand and waggles her long, graceful fingers, but whether she's showing him bites or imitating spider legs, he can't tell.

Nagle's smile is quick, rueful. He stares at the books, half-expecting little poisonous creatures to scurry out of them.

"Tell you what," she says. "Climb down and sit yourself in that chair, and see what you can make of those books. I'll be back directly." Then she leaves the room.

Descending carefully with the books in his arms, Nagle sits in the recliner, places the stack on his lap, and unpicks the knotted twine. The rope is ancient, and comes apart in his hands, which makes him feel like a scavenger brushing the last bits of nest off eggs he has stolen. He has never heard of C. Rossetti, so he takes the Bible first and sets the others on the coffee table beside him.

Right away, he notices the thinness, the lack of weight. The pages must be gossamer, he thinks, and gently pulls the covers apart. But the paper is sturdy, gilt-edged nineteenth century stock. There just isn't enough of it. Most of the contents have been cut away. The first page opens not with, *"In the beginning,"* but with, *"And he said unto me, Unto two thousand and three hundred days; then shall the sanctuary be cleansed."* The Book of Daniel, Nagle notes. The *"two thousand and three hundred days"* has been underscored in red ink three times, the third strike so emphatic that it stabbed through the paper. There is more under-lining in verse 9:24, beneath the phrase *"Seventy weeks are deter-mined upon thy people."* After the Book of Daniel comes Ezekiel, though Nagle spots no markings there. The rest is Revelation.

Nagle closes the book. He has never been a religious man; he has always been wary of God and churches alike. Both have the power to get inside you and take over your life completely.

The Rossetti book is also slim, slightly taller, and has been handled more gently or perhaps just less. Its cover is free of wear, of everything but dust. He opens to the title page:

MARY FROM THE COUNSELOR. CHRISTMAS 1872

So straight is the script of these words that Nagle squints closer to make sure they aren't some sort of cryptic subtitle. The letters are handwritten, straight up and down and perfectly level. His hostess returns carrying a tray with a teapot and one teacup and sets the plain, chip-free white china beside the books on the coffee table. She turns, grabs a long, black poker and prods the fire awake, then settles herself in the chair across from him, the poker in her lap.

"'I nursed it in my bosom while it lived,'" she says, looking at Nagle. "'I hid it in my heart when it was dead. In joy I sat alone; even so I grieved alone, and nothing said.'" She nods toward the book in his hands. Her smile is cold and impersonal; the smile she has always shown him. Nagle relaxes a bit.

"Poetry is still hard for me," he says.

"Not hard, unfamiliar," she says, her New England 'a' as tight and strangled as a constrictor-hitch. "All good poetry is unfamiliar at first, but usually simple enough, once you sort out where you are, what sort of company you're in. Take that one." She points to the book in his hands.

"Christina Rossetti."

She nods. "Sister of the much more celebrated Dante. He was one of those Pre-Raphaelites, lots of sylvan glades and shafts of sunlight, at least until his wife died. After that, he came a little unglued. Did you know he buried his wife with a sheaf of poems, then dug her up to get them back? He spent the rest of his days mourning and brooding and writing badly. But as for Christina..." His hostess traces the handle of the poker with her long fingers. "She was sane, even when she wrote about goblins. There's no trick to reading her poems, they're like watching her step naked right out of the book. Died horribly, though. Some kind of disease that twisted her up inside. They say she kept people awake for miles around, screaming in pain." She hooks Nagle's eyes with her own. "Still. It's better to die horribly than live horribly, given a choice. Don't you think?"

Once again, he finds himself uncertain how to respond. Loon call saves him, slashing over the unseen lake just beyond the windowless walls. "Seems like a moot question," he says when it's quiet again. "No one I know gets to choose when they suffer." He lifts his teacup and nearly drops it. Spiders unfold on the surface of the tea and then scuttle across it on their thin legs.

Only they aren't spiders, of course, and he blushes with the realization. Jasmine pods. Real jasmine. He and Elise had seen them once, when they took each other to the Russian Tea Room for their fifth anniversary. It was the sort of thing they'd always done, dared each other through doorways they never would have entered separately.

"Of course, my great-great-great grandmother Mary loved Rosetti's poems," his hostess says.

Nagle sips his tea, which is fragrant, strong. "How do you know?"

His hostess taps the first set of books he withdrew from the hiding place, and pulls them off the table into her lap. "It's quite a story. Would you like to hear it?"

Nagle has the distinct impression that this is all for show, that she has told this story dozens of times, but he nods anyway.

She slides a finger through the twine, which evaporates like smoke. Pulling the top volume onto her lap, she sets the poker aside and turns the pages. "There's a reference to Mary," his hostess begins, "in one of Thoreau's letters to Emerson. She did not become his laundress by accident, you see. She was the best-read person in the area, and she dreamed of teaching at Dartmouth one day, but of course that was all but unthinkable then. They heard tell of her, though—Hawthorne, Emerson, all of them—and she received a peculiar sort of advanced education through association. It didn't hurt that she was beautiful. Green eyes, white-blond hair, wild-looking for New England, and very small feet, which men always seem to find so reassuring."

Her glance isn't accusatory; she's just sizing him up. Nagle doesn't know how he feels about women's feet, but he has the disconcerting sense that his hostess believes she does.

"What did Thoreau say about Mary?" he asks. "In the letter to Emerson?"

"'Good God, Friend, what nature of marsh-sibyl have you unleashed on me?'"

Nagle laughs, though his hostess barely smiles.

"Emerson introduced them, you see. I guess he didn't mind straight feedback as much as your Thoreau."

"Or else small feet had a stronger effect on him."

At that, his hostess smiles, even inclines her chin. Then she drops her eyes to the book, and the smile disappears. Flatly, quietly, she begins to read.

"*April 11, 1842—Up they come from the Burned-Over District, more every year, until one wonders if they're growing them down there. Amusing to think about, a little gaggle of Millerites in their dark clothes and dark hats bowing their heads and knees to receive their fire and brimstone in some little farm church, and then slipping out back in the upper New York slush to tend to the new ones, the next generation, all staked and trussed and sprouting limbs along the back fence behind the graveyard like tomato plants. Did you know Miller himself is a farmer, or was? Anyway, they're here, and they've all but taken over the village, now. They've managed to enlist Tom Evans, the Whitesmiths, the whole Roberts clan, no big surprise there. Apparently, they know better than to come out here, or someone has told them. Maybe Little Ben Roberts is still reeling because I turned him down, and he's spreading tales of the unbeliever-witch in the cottage in the woods. Or maybe he's looking out for me. Either way, so much the better. Though I've seen one Millerite on the square over in Meredith, pointy black beard, wonderful black eyes, farmer's shoulders and a dreamer's face. Now there's a holy man this particular forest witch wouldn't mind luring to her lair. I'd be happy to give that one a taste of the End of the World . . .*

"*All right, the spring night has officially turned me wicked, and so I close. New book package from Gotham soon, maybe even this week.*"

Nagle remembers that he is holding his teacup and sets it down with a clink, which nevertheless seems loud. His hostess doesn't look up, just licks the end of a finger and turns the page. He shifts, winces as the chair squeaks, and decides he's enjoying this, even through the persistent anxiety he keeps trying to suppress.

"*August 4, 1842,*" his hostess begins again. "*Saw Cady Stanton over at the college today, speaking outside in the pouring rain.*

She didn't use an umbrella, but the rest of us did, and the drops sounded like drums beating right on top of our heads. She's from the Burned-Over, too, and you can tell. She waves her voice around like a torch and lights everyone up, although she had trouble getting us good and fired today, too dreary. I wonder if she likes to read. I bet she talks to writers all the time. Doesn't mean she enjoys books, though, and somehow it's hard to picture her sitting still long enough.

"The loons are leaving early this year. Too many Millerites, too much church bell ringing, I guess. So it's just me and the oak trees and some recopying work for Collins over in New Sandwich. There are so many acorns right now, they fall like hail."

More page turning, and Nagle, feeling hypnotized, asks, "How old was Mary when she was writing this?"

"Twenty-five, and she'd been on her own for the better part of nine years. Her parents were in the process of moving the family to one of those new Utopian experiments in Ohio, everyone living together in a big barn or some such, when they got sick and died on a farewell sight-seeing trip in the White Mountains. Not far from where your parents died, I believe."

Nagle grips the arms of the recliner. But he must have mentioned it to her at some point. Maybe that very first year. Even if he hadn't, his hostess surely would have heard about it. She was living here, then.

"February 27, 1843—A whole new batch of Millerites came pouring through the woods in covered wagons last night and descended on the town in the middle of a blizzard. I heard them in the notch not long after midnight, making such a clatter that I thought the moose, which have mostly disappeared from this forest, had come crashing back, and I rushed out to see them in my overcoat.

"My black-eyed boy's star must be rising, because he was the first one I saw, perched right on top of the front wagon next to the preachers in the big black hats. As they passed, he looked right through me as if I were a tree, winter-bare, not even there.

"In town today, I rousted Little Ben Roberts from the grain store, and he didn't want to be seen with me, but he told me why they're all gathered here and buzzing about. Apparently, they have a date.

Three weeks and two days from now, on April 3, 1843, the world will end by fire. Whether they're planning on starting the fire themselves or just dying in it, no one wants to say. As for me, I think Waldo better get busy cleaning out all those self-congratulatory bons mots *he's been sprinkling into his letters, lest the cataclysm comes and the Four Horsemen show up and believe he actually wrote like that."*

Desultory, his hostess turns another page while Nagle thinks of calling Elise. But he isn't sure he wants to hear her voice. His own embarrassment, disappointment, and anger had been at least as acute as hers back in 1996, the year they received medical confirmation from two different doctors that the Nagle line would end, because he was incapable of producing the necessary sperm count.

"April 3, 1843—Bright, slushy spring day. Black bears in the birches down by the river. More recopying to do. Four Horsemen absent. Sheep, loons, Robertses, Evanses, Millerites all present and accounted for.

"August 22, 1843—Mr. Miller, it seems, miscalculated. Counted Daniels as daffodils and daisies as days, and so came in a year or so wide. The actual date of our extinction is to be March 21st of next year. Much relief, bell ringing, and ceremonial robe buying amongst the Millerites.

"February 1, 1844—Even earlier than last year, they are back, preparing.

"February 22rd, 1844—He came. My black-eyed boy, in the flesh, at my door. Such a tormented face behind that pointed beard. Young Goodman B. himself, having walked straight off the page into my woods.

"'Come in,' I told him, and I would have said it was impossible seconds before, but his face got even sadder out there in the snow. And then—he spoke! Good Lord, he sounded like an owl, his voice all round and dark, too full for his body.

"'You come out,' he said. 'Here, with us, where it's safe.'

"I pointed out that, according to his people, the world was about to end, so how was that safe? If he saw a contradiction, he acknowledged none. But before he left, he turned around once more and looked at me,

*not through me this time, and said, 'YOU must come. YOU must see.'
And so I think maybe he has noticed me after all.*

"March 21, 1844—This time, the apocalypse started much more
promisingly. I was awoken at dawn by lightning so vicious that it
seemed to light the buds on the trees like candles, and the thunder that
followed literally hurled me from my bed. I dressed, draped a coat over
my head, and hurried through the woods, which rattled and rustled in
the rain as though some great host had indeed arisen within it. I'll
admit, there was a single moment, as the loons lifted all together,
wailing from the lake, when a tremor passed through me. But then, I got
to thinking how all this wet would make a heaven-sent, world-ending
fire that much more difficult to start, and I wanted to burst out singing.
I ran through the downpour.

"Town was eerily empty. I heard murmuring and chanting coming
from the church, so over I went. But they weren't inside. They were in
the graveyard. In the graves. Lord knows what they did with the
bones, because they'd dug up every inch of consecrated soil and then
leapt into the earth to wait. Whole families. People I know. Little Ben
Roberts and his sweet sister Sadie and his mother and father. It wasn't
funny, and I wasn't really laughing, I just couldn't think of what to say
or do. Someone threw a dirt clod and smashed me in the ear, so I
crouched in the mud.

"In the grave closest to me, a man I'd never seen before sat with his
children tucked against him, and to my astonishment, he had a
dripping wet copy of **The Sketch Book of Geoffrey Crayon** open in
his hands, and he was reading **Rip Van Winkle** aloud. He glanced up
at me, not unkindly.

"'Not quite the Bible,' I said.

"'It's a long way to Heaven,' he said. 'I thought the little ones
might get bored.'

"For the first time, then, I really was afraid. I got up, slipping and
stumbling away as fast as I could, and bumped headlong into my black-
eyed boy. He grabbed me about the shoulders, and I believed momentarily
that he meant to strangle me, but he steadied me instead and let go.

"'Will you join us?' he asked, his owl-voice dazzling, mournful,
overwhelming.

"'If you're right,' I said, 'I'll have no choice. For now, I still do.'
The sun had broken through the overcast even before I reached my
cottage door."

Nagle hasn't moved. He feels as though he's on one of those
fairground rides that spin so fast the g-force pins you against the
wall. Now, he wants to say something, but his hostess doesn't
look up.

"Quite a story, you're right," he finally tries.

Then she does. Her eyes are expressionless. She lifts the
diary and commences reading once more.

"July 7, 1844—Since the Disappointment—that's what they're
calling it—I have stayed out of town as much as possible. I have kept to
my books, which have given me less pleasure than usual, and I have
walked so long in the woods that even the bobcats no longer flee me. The
world hasn't ended. It just seems to have emptied."

"Two years on, now," his hostess says. "*June 4, 1846—My*
29th birthday. Two goshawks and one brave wren celebrated with me.
After the Disappointment, most of the Millerites scattered back to their
farms and families, and many left the area entirely. Alas, those that
have stayed are the ugliest and most stubborn remnant of the believers.
They huddle behind hedges when they see me coming, and today they
closed their shop windows in my face. I threw myself a picnic under the
oak tree in the town square for spite, then came home. At dusk, a knock
at my door startled me from my work desk. I considered fleeing or
hiding in the attic, but did neither. Instead, I marched through the hall
and flung open the door to find Little Ben R., pale and sad with his hat
in his hands, his beautiful yellow hair shining like daisies in the sun.

"'Mary-gold,' he said. He has called me that ever since our school
days.

"'Come in,' I told him, but he refused.

"'The day of the Dis…that stupid day at the church. I was the one
threw the mud at you. I was angry. I was crazy. I was wrong.'

"'Oh, Ben,' I said. 'You were always crazy. Always wrong.' And I
was so happy just to have him there that I tossed my arms around him
and kissed him on the cheek.

"*He leapt back and blushed as though I'd dropped my dress.*

'I'm going,' he said. 'To university, where I should have been all along. I just wanted to say goodbye to you, and now I've said it.' Then he bolted into the woods.

"I am going to die alone."

Gently, as though patting the hand of a child to bid it goodnight, his hostess closes the book.

"Shall I go on?" she says, opening the next volume in the stack

"Why did she stay here?" Nagle asks, as if the answer might explain why he has kept coming back, all this time.

"She doesn't say. But she had her work, her home. The people who valued her knew where to find her. She was wise enough, I suppose, to know that those things were more than anyone has a right to expect. So she did Thoreau's laundry, and biked eight miles to Holderness for her groceries, and kept out of town. Emerson invited her to work as a secretary at one of the universities in Boston and keep his family company, but she wrote back to say that someone had to keep an eye on the Millerites."

His hostess rests her hand on the open book like a little girl touching her reflection on the water. She is more alone than I am, Nagle thinks.

"January 1, 1855—They came today at dawn.

"Ten years ago—eight years ago, five, even—I might have expected it. But it has been so long. And last night, the snow came down soft and deep, covering my little porch, blanketing the trees and the forest floor, filling in all the terrible spaces in the world. I had rung in the New Year with my spirits—Nat's sad little twice-told ghosts, and the chokecherry cordial I bought from Richard Hart's wife over by Squam Lake. When the rapping and pounding came at the door, I was not only surprised but barely inside my body, having slipped safely down the well of sleep. Then Tom Evans, Jed Whitesmith, and a couple more I have known since before I was born burst into the room. There were others with them. Millerites, I assumed, or whatever they are calling themselves now that Miller had failed them. Even if I'd been fully awake and sober, I couldn't have fought them or run away, because they really had come

for me, and they really did want me.

"'Get dressed,' Tom Evans barked, looking at my wall sconce so he could pretend he hadn't seen my open robe.

"'What do you think you might do with me, then?' I asked.

"One of the Millerites looked up from under his wide, black hat, and Lord, he was only a boy, couldn't have been more than twelve. Not a hair on his face.

"'Save you,' he said, so sweetly.

"'For that, I'll need my walking dress,' I snapped, because by that point I had come back to myself, some. I splashed water on my face and put on layers of underclothing and my two sturdiest, plainest black dresses, one over the other. No reason to antagonize them further, I reasoned. And no need to be cold. They let me take a small satchel of necessaries and this diary, and that's all. My salvation, apparently, resides here, where I write by the single candle they have allotted me, in the newly built White Mountains Women's Asylum.

"Ah, well. The dark is dark, the sheets are clean, they have left me alone to write, none of my fellow inmates are screaming. I will wait for the light. Then I will see."

"Jesus," Nagle whispers.

"January 2, 1855—My head throbs as though it has been sawed open, the contents moved around to make room for all the revelations I am to receive.

"The strategy is this: I am to be denied sleep. Outside my cell door, they have hung a cowbell, as well as assorted metal implements. Every hour or so, someone comes and clangs the bell and rattles the bars until I bolt upright and throw my hands over my ears. Then the boy I saw yesterday or one of the others comes to me. They whisper without pause about the end of the world. I almost feel like an oracle, except that my head is cracking open. Then they leave me for a while. Brief while. Until the next round of clanging and rattling and visitations. Over and over. And now they have come again…

"January 8, 1855—Apparently, 1855 will be the year that Mary Elizabeth Gault will not sleep at all. It has been seven days. There is no pain anymore. My head has ceased to warn me of the dangers of unceasing consciousness. There is no sense anymore. I have screamed

at them, 'HAVE WE NOT BEEN THROUGH THIS? Did you all not bury yourselves once, and would you mind very much going off and doing it again?'

"I wonder what they're doing with my letters. They're not sending them, surely. Not that they need worry. Who would come?

"February 12, 1855—I got a walk today. Out to the edge of the woods and back. Snow thick on the ground, but I could not feel it. Ice trapping the light, so that the trees and the clouds and the little roofs looked abandoned. No birds, no deer, no winter loons. Only my own footprints, my keeper's alongside, his whispered words. The end is near. Bow down. Let go of your pride. Open your heart. Receive. Repent.

"March 1, 1855—Two months, today, by my still-running count in the dirt on the floor of my cell. This cannot last. They will have me. Or I will die. Or the undreamt dreams massing beneath my eyelids will burst over me in a torrent and carry me away and away. Please God, if there is a God, not to Heaven. The light is too bright, and I must sleep."

His hostess offers another of those close-lipped, fleeting smiles. "After that, the entries are less frequent, more disjointed, and little wonder. At one point, she considers running, but to where, or whom? And anyway, she no longer has the strength. And then—"

"Stop," Nagle says, his voice edgy, nastier than he intended. His limbs feel weighted, as though the blood has pooled and thickened inside them. "Wait. Please."

She doesn't look up, but waits.

"I mean…how does someone just fall out of the world, and no one notices?"

"You're not enjoying my story, are you, Mr. Nagle? Well. It's almost over. *June 4, 1857—They have made a tactical error. Did they know it was my birthday? I feel as though I have had a snowball smashed in my face, that my poor, sun-starved birth skin has split and fallen from me. They have brought me books, and I am born anew, strong like they will never be. How did they even manage it? Did Tom Evans take pity on me after all this time? It is more than two years since they have imprisoned me here. They almost never come to talk to me anymore, and they may not realize it, but they probably need not ring the bell or clang the bars of my cell any longer. I could no more sleep through an hour than freeze myself into ice and melt through the floor with the morning sun.*

"Somehow, they have located Little Ben Roberts, now married and settled somewhere near Keene, a father twice over, and a bookseller! They have told him that I am ill and enduring a long, private convalescence. And he has remembered what I love—or at least what I loved when he knew me—and has sent me treasure beyond what I could ever have hoped. Hello, Pamela, you stupid, sullen, virtuous ass. Hello, Henry David, you self-righteous so-and-so. I have missed you terribly.

"My jailers say they want to remind me—in case they have accidentally made me forget—what the merciful love of a gracious God can inspire a man to do. They say they want to enlighten me, not crush me. On that score, they needn't worry now. With these books, I can build a fortress through which none can reach me. Farewell, Jesus. Go ahead and end the world without me.

"Winter, 1859—Somewhere, I lost track of a day, or several. I have given up guessing. What does it matter? What matters is this: they are letting me out in the evenings, like a half-domesticated cat, to roam the woods and hills alone. They have asked only for assurance that I will not run, and I have given it gladly. I no longer want to run. They don't realize what has happened to me. I stop under a tree, and crows cease cawing. The drifted snow scrapes up my legs and down into my boots, but it does not—cannot—make me cold. The moon moves where I tell it. In the shadows of the firs, I have sensed bobcats shadowing me. The Millerites do not know what they have made from me. I cannot be killed from lack of sleeping. Forgive them, Lord. I'll never.

"I have banished sleep altogether. It has been seventeen days since I so much as closed my eyes. I read, I walk, I have waking dreams. What a strange drowsiness possesses them, all these Millerites and townspeople. Whereas my little life is rounded by nothing. Grounded by nothing. Bounded by nothing.

"The Counselor came today."

Nagle leans forward and takes a gulp of cold tea, the jasmine pods drowned and limp on the surface. The aftertaste burns the back of his throat, and he coughs hard. The cup clatters in the saucer, and a single loon lets loose one of those longer, climbing cries, a whole throat flung open to the sky. He hears crickets. An owl. The lake lapping against the dock in the inky blackness of the New Hampshire night, just out of sight beyond this windowless room.

"If Mary kept a diary of the 1860s," his hostess says, "no one has ever found it. And in the last volume—" she holds up the book with the spine that reads *1870* "—there is just the one entry. *June 4, 1871—I am daydreaming today—for sleep is a whole other country now—about the evening he came back to me. Rail-thin in his long, black robe, a boy no longer, his lovely lips lost in the black bramble of his beard. He came trailing Millerites like trained hounds behind him, but entered my asylum alone and took me out for a walk. For nearly one hour—the time I once measured in snatched sleep—we did not speak.*

"*Finally, I stopped beneath an oak tree, heard a branch bend above, and knew that one of my companions had arrived to watch us.*

"*'Have you come to free me?' I asked.*

"*''Twas I who had you brought here,' he said. 'So you could free yourself.'*

"*'And so I have,' I told him. He didn't respond. His eyes were as black as a wolverine's, and just as wary. I asked his name.*

"*Then he sighed, and for a moment, he was my boy again, and those eyes drank me in, and I drank, too. Here, I thought, was a force of the forest, something to lure to my bed and keep beside me, both of us burning bright to warm the terrifying cold out of the other.*

"*'Why, woman? Why will you not yield? How can you, who sees and knows so much, not see what is right in front of you?'*

"*I sensed my advantage and pressed it the best way I knew how: I took his hand. It lay in my palm like a trembling chick. I could feel his sweat. The first proof, in so long, of my own heat.*

"*'How can you still be sure?' I whispered, the bracken on his face all but tickling my cheek. 'In spite of the Disappointment, the disappearance of your flock, the feelings I can feel, right now, stirring in your skin. How can you believe that the world is about to end?'*

"*His hand slipped from mine like a brook trout wriggling free of the* hook, and his wolverine eyes rocked me in my birth of bone and breath. 'Because I am the Counselor,' he said. 'And I have come to end it.' And with that, he left me there.

"Once a month, ever since, and sometimes more, the Counselor comes to take me walking. Always, he brings my latest package from Little Ben, who apparently has cast aside his wild religion and become a devotee of wild British poetry. He sends me Morris, Swinburne, the Rossettis. The Counselor tells me of the impending glories of the new Coming, when the earth and lakes and undeserving will burn away in a single blast, leaving the blessed to proceed in company and song to Glory. I walk closer to him than he wants me to, and I stoke my smile constantly to keep it bright, because if it should slip, flicker, fail…

"Sometimes, I think about the world beyond this valley, over the White Mountains. The world of waking and sleeping and dreaming and not believing. The world I once was certain was my own. Dream on, I say to that world. Sleep well. And I will stay. Because either the Counselor and I have both been driven to madness by decades among the Millerites—perfectly possible, and please God, let it be so—or I am Scheherazade, dancing and bantering, flirting and teasing, so that the Counselor never realizes that the last task he set himself to complete before ending the world was accomplished a decade ago. Because I swear I felt it in his skin, the moment I touched him. I saw it flicker in the blackness of his eyes. And still, he has never realized that I believe him. To him, I remain the forest witch he has imprisoned and will never admit he loves. The one whom he apparently cannot proceed to Heaven without.

"Meanwhile, you Millerites. Sleep, also. All you Evanses, Whitesmiths, and Nagles who brought me here. Dream of the day it is finished, one way or the other, and one of us comes for you in the dark."

Closing the book, his hostess looks up and cocks her head on her long, white neck as Nagle twitches, helpless, in his chair. "That's it," she says, as that cryptic smile slips across her face again, then disappears. "Drink it all in, now." She stands. "You see, it's become a sort of family tradition. Passed down from generation to generation. The obliteration of the lot of you—the ones who imprisoned her—one family at a time.

And since I'm now 54—the age Mary turned on the day of her last entry—and seeing as how you seem to have recovered at least some of your equilibrium a bit more quickly than I'd hoped.... But then maybe you didn't want children as much as you thought you did."

Gaping, Nagle twists and whimpers in his chair, remembering the night he woke up screaming, right upstairs, his abdomen blazing as though a poker had been stabbed through it, his testicles on fire. Good God, what had she done? He remembers Elise hurtling downstairs for the doctor. How long afterward had they discovered that he was sterile? Six months? Less?

Struggling against the constriction in his lungs, the intensifying weight of the air, Nagle gulps enough breath to say, "You murdered my parents."

"Oh, not me," she says, the moonlight shimmering behind her as she stands. "That was my mother. On her 54th birthday. Thirty-one years ago today, right? She had more of a...dramatic flair, I think. See, there are so few of you left. We try to keep it to one per generation, now."

The crushing sensation engulfs him, no longer in the air but like a fist around his heart. He can barely muster the energy to keep his head up.

"How?" he says feebly.

Her frown seems genuine, bemused. "I've often wondered. I mean, if the Counselor really was the man they both believed he was, how could Mary have withstood him all those years, as I assume she must have, since we're all still here? Unless she had some sort of extraordinary power of her own. Or maybe she was mad, but courageously so, with the kind of courage that allows someone to go it utterly alone in the face of a vindictive world."

She begins to circle the library, turning down lamps. Nagle closes his eyes as his compressed heart thumps and shudders.

"On the other hand," his hostess murmurs. "Just for fun. Think about all that power Mary had, whatever it was. Think about the Counselor's power, which at the very least was enough to convince hundreds, maybe thousands, that the kingdom of Heaven was at hand. Then think about those powers combined. Because surely by now you've figured out who my great-great-great grandfather was."

But Nagle is barely listening. When she closes the library door, he finds the darkness less consuming than he was expecting, more gray than black, and not entirely empty. He wonders if he will be buried beside his parents. Then he wonders if his parents are buried beside the last generation of the Evans family, the Whitesmiths, the rest of them. Maybe they have all been laid in that very same churchyard, in the very same graves where their ancestors waited bravely, joyfully, for the end of the world. Maybe he has come home.

Flowers on Their Bridles, Hooves in the Air

"Mechanical constructions designed for pleasure have a special melancholy when they are idle. Especially merry-go-rounds."
—Wright Morris

Ash came in late, on the 10:30 train. I was sure Rebecca would stay home and sleep, but instead she got a sitter for our infant daughter, let her dark hair down for what seemed the first time in months, and emerged from our tiny bathroom in the jeans she hadn't been able to wear since her Ceasarean.

"My CD," she said happily, handing me the New York Dolls disc she'd once howled along with every night while we did the dishes, and which I hadn't even seen for over a year. Then she stood in front of me and bobbed on the clunky black shoes I always loved to see her in, not because they were sexy but because of their bulk. Those shoes, it seemed to me, could hold even Rebecca to the ground.

So all the way across the San Fernando Valley we played the Dolls, and she didn't howl anymore, but she rocked side-to-side in her seat and mouthed the words while I snuck glances at her in the rearview mirror. The last time I could remember seeing her in this mood was on her thirty-first birthday, over a year ago, right before her mother died and the homeless persons' political action committee she'd been serving on collapsed in the wake of 9/11. Right at the moment she'd finally decided to give up on the rest of the world long enough for us to try to have a child.

I had thought maybe this Rebecca—arms twitching at her sides like folded wings, green eyes skimming the night for anything alive—had vanished for good.

As usual, even at that hour, traffic snarled where the 101 and the 110 and the 5 emptied together into downtown Los Angeles, so I ducked onto Hill Street, edging us through the surprising crowds of Chinese teens tossing pop-pops in the air and leaning against lampposts and chain-shuttered shop windows to smoke. Rebecca rolled down her window, and the car filled with burning smells: tobacco, firecracker filament, pork, and fish. I thought she might try bumming a cigarette from a passing kid—though as far as I knew, she hadn't smoked in years—but instead she leaned against the seatback and closed her eyes.

We were pulling into Union Station when she turned the volume down, caught me looking at her in the mirror, and said, "A flowered one."

I grinned back, shook my head. "He's a new man, remember? Official, responsible, full-time job. Brand new lakefront bungalow. He'll be wearing gray pinstripes. From a suit he bought but hasn't worn."

We were both wrong. And of course, the funniest thing—the worst—was that even with all that green and purple paisley flashing off the front of this latest vest like scales on some spectacular tropical fish, I still didn't see him until I'd driven ten yards past him.

"Hey, dude," he said to both of us as he approached the car, then dropped his black duffel to the curb and stood quietly, leaning to the right the way he always did.

He'd shaved off the last of the tumbling dark brown curls which, even thinning, used to flop over both his eyes and made him look like a lhasa apso. Even more brightly than the new vest, the top of his head shone, practically winking white and red with the lights from passing cars. His shoulders, big from the boxing classes he took—for fitness, he'd never gotten in a ring and swore he never would—ballooned from either side of the vest. His jeans were black, and on his wrists were leather bracelets studded with silver spikes.

"Ash, you, um," I said, and then I was laughing. "You don't *look* like a nurse."

"Wait," Rebecca said, and her hand snaked out the window and grabbed the side of Ash's vest, right where the paisley met the black polyester backing. Then she popped her seatbelt open and leaned to look more closely. "Did you do this?"

Ash's blush spread all the way up his head until he was red all over, and his tiny ferret-eyes blinked. It was as though Rebecca had spray-painted him.

"Do what?"

"What *was* this?" Rebecca said. "Was this a shirt?"

"What do you mean?"

"Look, El. Someone cut this shiny paisley part off...curtains, maybe? Something else, anyway. And then stitched it to the rest. See?" She held the edge of the vest out from Ash's sides.

Ash's blush deepened, but his smile came more easily than I remembered. "No wonder it cost a dollar."

Rebecca burst out laughing, and I laughed, too. "Been way too long, Ash," I said.

Still leaning, as though he were standing in some invisible rowboat in a current, Ash folded himself into our Metro's tiny back seat. "Good to be here, Elliot." He pronounced it El-yut, just as he had when we were twelve.

"You get all dolled up for us?" I said, nodding in the mirror at the vest, and to my surprise, Ash blushed again and looked at the floor.

"I've been going out a lot," he said.

Both he and Rebecca left their windows open as I spun the car out of the lot and, without asking, turned south. With Chinatown behind us, the street corners emptied. I couldn't see the smog, but I could taste it, a sweet tang in the air that shouldn't have been there and prickled the lungs like nicotine and had a similar sort of narcotic, addictive effect, because you just kept gulping it. Of course, that was partially because there wasn't enough oxygen in it.

"Where are you going?" Rebecca asked as we drifted down the white and nameless warehouses that line both sides of

Alameda Street and house the city's *other* industries, whatever they are.

"Don't know," I said. "Just figured, between Ash's vest and your mood, home wasn't an option."

Rebecca twisted her head around to look at Ash. "Where's all this *out* you've been going?"

"Meditation classes, for one," Ash said, effectively choking Rebecca to silence. She'd forgotten about Ash's professed Zen conversion, or discovery, or whatever it was. He'd told us about it in a particularly cryptic phone call that had struck both of us as dispassionate even for Ash. Yet another 9/11 by-product, we both thought at the time, but now I actually suspected not. Even back in our Berkeley days, Ash's sense of right and just behavior had been more…inward, somehow, than Rebecca's.

Also less ferocious. He hadn't actually believed he could affect change, or maybe wasn't as interested in doing so, and was therefore less perpetually disappointed. And now, as we floated between late-night trucks down the dark, toward the freeways, a series of quick, sweet feelings lit up inside me like Roman candles. I was remembering Friday nights lost in Oakland, gliding through streets emptier and darker than this in Ash's beat-up green B-210, singing "Shoplifters of the World," spending no money except on gas and Bongo Burgers.

"I've been going to music, too. Lots of clubs. My friends Rubina and Liz—"

"Long Beach," Rebecca said over him, and I hit the brakes and paused, right on the lip of the onramp to the 10. Whether out of perceptiveness or meditation training or typical Ashy patience, our friend in the back went quiet and waited.

"Rebecca," I said carefully, after a long breath. She'd been taking us to her sister's almost every weekend since her mother died. She'd been going during the week, too, of late, and even more than she told me, I suspected. "Don't you want to get Ash a Pink's? Show him that ant at the Museum of Jurassic Tech? Take him bowling at the Starlight? Show him the Ashy parts of town?"

"Starlight's gone," Rebecca said, as though she were talking about her mother.

"Oh, yeah. Forgot."

Abruptly, she brightened again. "Not my sister's, El-yut. I have a plan. A place in mind. Somewhere our vested nurse-boy back there will appreciate. You, too." Then she punched play on the CD player. Discussion over. Off we went.

All the way down the 110, then the 405, Rebecca alternately shook to the music and prodded Ash with questions, and he answered in his familiar monotone, which always made him sound at ease, not bored, no matter what job he'd just left or new woman he'd found and taken meditating or clubbing or drifting and then gotten gently dumped by. Ash had been to more weddings of more ex-girlfriends than anyone I'd ever met.

But tonight, he talked about his supervisor at the hospital, whose name apparently really was Ms. Paste. "She's kind of this nurse-artist," he said. "Amazing. Hard to explain. She slides an I.V. into a vein and steps back, and it's perfect, every time, patient never even feels it. Wipes butts like she's arranging flowers."

Rebecca laughed, while Ash sat in the back with that grin on his face. How can someone so completely adrift in the world seem so satisfied with it?

We hit the 710, and immediately, the big rigs surrounded us. No matter what hour you drive it, there are always big rigs on that stretch of highway, lumbering back and forth between the 405 and the port, their beds saddled with giant wooden crates and steel containers newly gantried off incoming ships or headed for them, as though the whole city of Long Beach were constantly being put up or taken down like a circus at a fairground. As we approached the fork where the freeway splits—the right headed for the Queen Mary, the left for Shoreline Village and the whale-watching tour boats and the too-white lighthouse perched on its perfectly mown hilltop like a Disneyland cast-off—I slowed and glanced at my wife. But Rebecca didn't notice. She'd slid down a little in her seat and was watching the trucks with a blank expression on her pale face.

"Rebecca?" I said. "Where to?"

Stirring, she said, "Oh. The old pier. You know where that is? Downtown, downtown."

Just in time, I veered left, passing by the aquarium and the rest of the tourist attractions to head for the city center. Not that there was much difference anymore, according to Rebecca. Scaffolding engulfed most of the older buildings, and as we hit downtown, the bright, familiar markings of malls everywhere dropped into place around us like flats on a movie set. There were Gap and TGIF storefronts, sidewalks so clean they seemed to have acquired a varnish, fountains with statues of seals spouting water through their whiskers. Only a few features distinguished this part of Long Beach from the Third Street Promenade or Old Town Pasadena now: a *tapas* bar; that eighty-year-old used bookshop with the bowling alley-sized backroom that seemed to exude dust through the wood and windows, even though the windows were painted shut; and, just visible down the last remaining dark blocks, a handful of no-tourist dives with windowless doors and green booths inside for the more traditionally-minded sailors.

"Go straight through," Rebecca said. "Turn right at the light. God, it's been years."

Given her tastes and the sheer number of days she'd spent with her mother here, then more recently with her sister, that seemed unlikely. But Ash's patience was soothing, infectious. I waited. And as we edged farther from the downtown lights, through sports cars and SUVs skimming the streets like incoming seagulls and squawking at each other over parking places, Rebecca shut off the music and turned to us. "My dad used to take us here," she said.

I hit the brakes harder than I meant to and brought the car to a lurching stop at the road that fronted the ocean. For a few seconds, we hung there, the lights of Long Beach in the rearview mirror, the ocean seeping blackly out of the jumbled, overbuilt coast before us like oil from a listing tanker.

"Your dad," I said.

"Left, Elliot. Down there. See?"

I turned left, slowly, though there was no traffic. Neither tourists nor sailors had any use for this road anymore, apparently. "It's been a long time since you mentioned your dad," I said. In fact, I couldn't remember the last time. She talked about her school-commissioner mother: stable, stubborn, fiercely loyal, nasty Scrabble player. Also her recovered junkie sister. But her father...

"I've never heard you mention him," Ash said, detached as ever.

The frontage road, at least, did not look like new downtown Long Beach, or Third Street, or Downtown Disney. To our left, the scaffolded buildings loomed, lightless as pilings for some gigantic pier lost long ago to the tide. To our right lay the ocean, without even a whitecap to brighten its surface. Few other stretches in the LosAnDiego megalopolis were still allowed to get this dark. We'd gone no more than a few hundred yards when Rebecca sat up in her seat and pointed.

"Right here. See?"

I punched the brakes again and brought the car to a stop. Just behind us, a sign-less, potholed drive snaked between the black iron posts of what must once have been a gate. Beyond that, I saw a parking lot, then the old pier, lit by dim streetlights on either side. And beyond those, right at the end of the pier...

"What is that?" Ash said.

It seemed to hover above the ocean, a dark, metallic, upside-down funnel, like a giant magician's hat. Beneath it, dim and scattered lights flickered. If there were ocean rather than pier beneath it, I would have assumed we were looking at bioluminescent fish.

I glanced toward Rebecca, whose smile was the wistful one I'd gotten used to over the past year or so. When I reached over and squeezed her hand, she squeezed back, but absently.

"What's the smile for?" I said, and turned us into the drive. Past the gateposts, we emerged into a startlingly large parking lot that sprawled in both directions. A handful of older cars—

an orange Dodge pickup, a '60s-vintage Volkswagen van, a U-haul trailer with no lead-vehicle attached to it—clustered like barnacle shells near the foot of the wooden steps that led up to the pier. Otherwise, there were only empty spaces, their white dividing lines obscured but still visible, rusted parking meters planted sideways at their heads like markers on anonymous graves.

"There used to be a billboard right next to that gate," Rebecca said, staring around her. "A girl dressed in one of those St. Pauli Girl waitress uniforms, you know what I'm talking about? Breasts like boulders, you felt like they were going to pop loose and roll right off the sign and smash you when you drove under them. She was riding one of the merry-go-round horses and holding a big beer stein. Her uniform said *Lite-Your-Line* on it, and in huge red letters over her head, the sign read, *LONG BEACH PIER. GET LIT.*"

Ash laughed quietly as I pulled into a spot a few rows from the van and pick-up, and Rebecca got out fast and stood into a surprising sea wind. Ash and I joined her, and I had a brief but powerful desire to ditch our friend, never mind how good it was to see him, take my wife by the elbow and steer her to the dark, disused stretch of beach fifty yards ahead of us. There we'd stand, and let the planet's breath beat against our skin until it woke us. The whole last year, it seemed to me, we'd been sleeping. Or I'd been sleeping, and Rebecca had been mourning, and something else, too. Retreating, maybe, from everything but her daughter.

"I think this is the only place I remember coming with him," Rebecca said. "For fun, anyway." She moved off toward the steps. We followed. Ash's vest left little purple trails of reflected streetlight behind him. His gaze was aimed straight up the steps. Rebecca had a deeper hunger for these spots, I thought, these night places where people washed up or swept in like sharks from the deep sea. But Ash could smell them.

"You came here a lot?" I asked. I considered taking Rebecca's hand again, but thought that would be crowding her, somehow.

"More than you'd think." She mounted the stairs. "Some days, he hadn't even started drinking, yet. He'd wait until we got here. Buy my sister and me each three dollars' worth of tickets—that was like fifteen rides—and plop us on the merry-go-round while he—"

The hands closed around us so fast, from both sides, that we didn't even have time to cry out. One second we were alone at the top of the leaning staircase and the next there were filthy fingers clamped on all of our wrists and red, bearded faces leering into ours. The fingers began dragging us around in a sickening circle.

"*Ring around the funny,*" the face nearest to me half-sang, his breath overwhelming, equal parts bad gin and sea salt and sand. "*Pockets full of money. Give it. Give it. Give it NOW!*"

Then, as suddenly as they had grabbed us, they let go, a hand or two at a time, fell back a step, and we got our first good look. If we hadn't been on a glorified dock at the edge of the Pacific, a hundred yards that felt like fifty miles from anywhere I knew, I think I might have laughed, or wept.

They stood before us in a clump, five decrepit men in ruined peacoats with their noses running and their beards wild and their skin mottled with sores red and raised like octopus suckers. Probably, I thought, Long Beach—like the former People's Republic of Santa Monica, and every other Southern California town I knew—had passed and enforced a new set of vagrancy laws to keep all that fresh sidewalk pavement free of debris. And this particular quintet had scuttled down here to hide under the great steel magician's hat and sleep with the fishes and pounce on whatever drifted out to them.

"Here," Ash started, sliding a hand into the pocket of his vest, just as Rebecca stuck an arm across his chest.

"Don't," she said.

It shouldn't have surprised me. I'd watched her do this before. Rebecca had worked with the homeless most of her adult life, and felt she knew what they needed, or at least what might be most likely to help. But I was always startled by the confidence of her convictions.

"Nearest shelter's on La Amatista," she said, gesturing over her shoulder toward the frontage road, town. "Five, maybe six blocks. They have food."

"Don't want food," one of the men snarled, but his snarl became a whine before he'd finished the sentence. "We want change."

"You won't get ours."

"*Change.*" The five of them knotted together—coiled, I thought, and my shoulders tensed, and I could feel the streaky wetness they'd left on my wrists and their breath in my mouth—and then, just like that, they were gone, bumping past us down the steps to disappear under the dock.

For a good minute, maybe more, the three of us stood in our own little clump. There were unsettled feelings seeping up through my stomach, and I could neither place them nor get them quiet. Finally, Rebecca said, "The most amazing merry-go-round," as though nothing whatsoever had occurred.

I glanced down the pier toward the magician's hat, which was actually the roof of an otherwise open pavilion. There were lights clustered beneath it, yellow and green and red, but they seemed to waver above the water, connected to nothing, until I realized I was looking through some sort of threadbare canvas drapery suspended from the rim of the overhang like a giant spider web, generations in the making. Between us and the pavilion lay maybe fifty yards of moldy wooden planking. Shadows of indeterminate shape slid over the planks or sank into them, and on either side of the streetlights, solitary figures sat at the railing-less edges and dangled their legs over the dark and fished.

"Is this safe, Rebecca?" I asked.

She'd seemed lost in thought, staring after our would-be muggers, but now she brightened again, so fast I got dizzy. "We'll let Ash go first. Drive everyone back with the vest." She flicked his front with her fingers, and I felt a flicker of jealousy, couldn't believe I was feeling it, and made myself ignore it.

Of course, Ash did go first. The lights and the pavilion and the curtain floating on the wind drew him. Me, too, but not in the same way. Rebecca waited for me to return her smile, then shrugged and stepped off behind our friend. I followed.

"They used to sell T-shirts from a stand right there," she said as we walked, gesturing at the empty space to her left. "Army camouflage. American flag prints. They sold candy popcorn, too. My dad always bought us the Patriotic Bag. Red cherry, blue raspberry, vanilla."

"Are there such things as blue raspberries?" Ash asked, but Rebecca ignored him.

"Lot of patriotic stuff, come to think of it. I wonder why. Bicentennial, maybe?"

If she was asking me, I had no answer. Periodically, one of the streetlamps buzzed or flickered. No moon. Our footsteps echoed strangely on the wet wood, sounding lighter than they should have. Not one of the fishermen glanced our way, though one twitched as we drew abreast, hunched forward to work furiously at his reel, and yanked a small ray right up into the air in front of him. It hung there streaming, maybe a foot across, its underside impossibly white, silently flapping. Like the ripped-out soul of a bird, I thought, and shuddered while the fisherman drew the ray toward him and laid it, gently across his lap. It went on flapping there until it died.

We'd all stopped in our tracks at the fisherman's first movements, and we stayed there quite a while. Eventually, Ash turned to us and nodded his head. "I have missed you, Rebecca," he said. "You, too, Elliot." But he meant Rebecca. He'd always meant Rebecca, and had told me so once, the night before graduation, on one of the rare occasions when he got high, just to see. "Count on you, I do," he'd told me. "Worship her."

Tonight, Rebecca didn't respond, and eventually Ash started toward the pavilion and the lights beneath it. We followed. I walked beside my wife, close enough for elbow contact but not manufacturing any. Something about the flapping ray reminded me of our daughter, squirming and jerking as she scrabbled for a hold in the world, and I wanted to be back at our house. In spite of the calmer, sadder way Rebecca had been this past year—maybe even because of it, though I hated thinking that—I loved our home.

"What made the merry-go-round so amazing?" I asked.

"The guy who designed it—Rooff, I think?—he's like the most famous American carousel builder. Or one of. He did this one in Rhode Island or Vermont, when they broke it up and sold off the horses, they went on eBay for $25,000 a piece. But this one..."

In the quiet of the next few seconds, I became aware, for the first time since we'd reached the pier, of the sounds. That wind, first of all, sighing out of the blackness to crash against the fortified city and then roll back. The ocean, shushing and muttering. The boards creaking as fishermen shifted or cast and seagulls dropped out of the dark to perch on the ruined railings. And, from straight ahead, under that darkly gleaming steel hat, an incongruous and unidentifiable tinkling, almost musical, barely audible, like an ice cream truck from blocks away.

"You should have seen their faces, Elliot. You would have loved them."

I blinked, still seeing the ray. "Really?"

"Rooff—the designer—he made them after his business partner died. His best friend, I guess. To keep himself company or something. I met this older man from the Carousel Preservation Assemblage who—"

"The Carousel what?" I said, and smiled. It really was astonishing, the people Rebecca knew.

"I met him at that open city planning meeting down here a couple years ago. The one about the development of the rest of downtown? The one I came home so upset from?"

"That would be every city planning meeting," I said. My smile faded, and the musical tinkling from the end of the pier got just a little louder.

"Anyway. These horses, Elliot. They were just...the *friend-*

liest horses I've ever seen. They all had huge dopey smiles on their faces. Their teeth either pointed out sideways, or else they were perfect and glowing. Their sides were shiny brown or black or pink or blue. Their manes all had painted glass rubies and sapphires sticking out of them, and the saddles had these ridiculously elaborate roses and violets carved into the seats. Hooves flying, like they just couldn't stand to come down, you know? Like it was too much fun just sailing around in a circle forever. The Preservation guy said Rooff installed every single one of them, and every cog of every machine down here, by himself, at night, by candlelight. As some kind of tribute to his friend or something. Said he was a total raving loon, too. Got involved in all kinds of séances trying to contact his friend after he died. Wound up getting publicly ridiculed by Harry Houdini, who broke up one of his little soirees, apparently. Died brokenhearted and penniless."

"Your kind of guy," I said. And I thought I understood, suddenly and for the first time, just how badly Rebecca's father had hurt her. Because he'd been her kind of guy, too.

Unlike me.

"Yep," said Rebecca, and her face darkened again. Her mood seemed to change with every breath now, like the pattern of shadows on the pier around us. "Anyway, this is where we came. My dad'd plop us on the merry-go-round, hand the operator a fistful of tickets, and there we'd stay while he went and…well. I'm not going to tell you."

Ahead, Ash reached the hanging drapes, which, up close, were stained and ratty and riddled with runs. Without turning around or pausing, he slipped inside them. Instantly, his form seemed to waver, too, just like the lights, as though he'd dived into a pool. I stopped, closed my eyes, felt the salt on my skin and smelled fish and whitewater. And smog, of course. Even here.

"Why won't you tell me?"

"Because I'm pretty sure you're going to get to see." She passed through the drapes, and I followed.

I don't know what I was expecting under the hat, but whatever it was, I was disappointed. The space under there was cavernous, stretching another thirty yards or so out to sea, but most of it was empty, just wood planking and the surrounding shroud flapping in the wind like the clipped and tattered wings of some giant ocean bird. Albatross, maybe. At the far end of the space, another white curtain, this one heavier and opaque, dropped from rafters to dock, effectively walling off what had to be the last few feet of pier and giving me uneasy thoughts about the Wizard of Oz behind his screen. A mirror-ball dangled overhead, gobbling up the light from the fixtureless hanging bulbs suspended from the rafters and shooting off the red and green and blue sparks I'd seen from down the pier.

Spaced around the perimeter of the enclosure, and making the tinkling, bleeping noises we'd heard from outside, were six or seven pre-video arcade games, and stationed at the one directly across from us, elbowing each other and bobbing up and down, were two kids, neither older than seven, both with startlingly long white-blonde hair pouring down their backs like melting wax. The one on the left wore a dress, the one on the right jeans. Of Rebecca's grinning horses, the only possible remnant was the room's lone attendant, who was hovering near the kids but looked up when we entered and shuffled smoothly away from them, head down, as though we'd caught him peeping at a window.

"Come here," Ash said, standing over one of the machines to our left. "Look at this."

We moved toward him, and as we did, the attendant straightened and began to scuttle over the planking toward us. Despite his surprising grace, he looked at least a hundred years old. His skin was yellow and sagging off his cheeks, his hair white and patchy. His shoulders dipped, seemingly not quite aligned with his waist, and his fingers twitched at the fringes of his blue workman's apron. It was as though nothing on that body quite fit, or had been his originally; he'd just found the shed exoskeleton and slipped inside it like a hermit crab. I couldn't take my eyes from him until he stopped in the center of the room.

"Hey," Rebecca said to Ash. "You're good."

"*Sssh*," Ash murmured, "Almost got it. *Shoot.*" There was a clunk from the machine, and I stepped up next to him.

"We had one of these at the 7-Eleven by my house," I said.

Simple game. You stuck your hands inside the two outsized, all-but-immovable gloves on the control panel. The gloves controlled a sort of crane behind the glass of the machine. You tried to maneuver the crane down to the pile of prizes encased in clear, plastic bubbles below, grab a bubble in the jaws of the crane, then lift and drop it down a circular chute to the left. If you got the bubble in the chute, it popped out to you, and you claimed your prize. I couldn't remember ever seeing anyone win that game.

"Let me try," said Rebecca, and slid a quarter into the slot and her hands into the gloves. She got the crane's jaws around a bubble with a jiggly rubber tarantula inside and dropped it before she got it anywhere near the chute's mouth.

"I'm going again," Ash said, slotting home another quarter.

Behind us, the attendant wriggled two steps closer. His hands fumbled at the work apron, and I finally noticed the change dispenser belted around his waist and rattling like a respirator. The thing was huge, ridiculous, had to have housed fifty dollars' worth of quarters, and could probably accommodate ten years' worth of commerce on this pier, given the traffic I'd seen tonight. The man looked at me, and a spasm rolled up his arms—or maybe it was a gesture. An invitation to convert some money.

"*Fucksicle*," Ash said, kneeing the machine as another plastic bubble crashed back to the pile.

"Now, now," I said, reaching for both his and Rebecca's shoulders, wanting to shake free of the attendant's gaze, and also of the mood I could feel rolling up on all of us like a tide. "Is that the Middle Path? The elimination of desire or whatever—"

"Don't you mock that," Ash snarled, half-shoving me as he

whirled around. His face had gone completely red again, and at his sides his fists had clenched, and I wondered if some of the assumptions Rebecca and I had been making—about whether he'd actually been in a boxing ring, for example—weren't years out of date.

Startled, shaking a little, I held up a hand. "Hey," I said. "It's just me. I wasn't—"

"Yes you were," Rebecca said, and my mouth fell open, to defend myself, maybe, at least from my wife who had no right, and then she added, "We both were. Sorry, Ash."

"I'm used to it," he said, in his normal, expressionless voice, and wandered away toward the next machine.

For a while, Rebecca and I stood, not touching, watching our friend. I hated when Rebecca went still like this: head cocked, hands in her pockets, green eyes glazed over. At least right now she was doing it during an argument, and not over breakfast coffee, in the midst of reading the paper, just because. Daphne, having sickened of being chased, turning herself into a tree.

Finally, I blew out the breath I hadn't realized I'd been holding and said, "You're wrong, Rebecca. You both are."

"Oh come on, Elliot. Even when he's not around, what do we talk about when we talk about Ash? His vests, and his inability to land a life-partner, and his refusal or whatever it is to hold a job, and the crazy situations he seems to wind up in without even trying, and—"

"There's a difference between enjoying and mocking."

That stopped her, and even unlocked her, a little. At least she re-cocked her head so it was facing me. "You enjoy us too much," she said, and followed Ash.

I was angry, then, and I didn't go after them immediately. I watched Rebecca approach Ash, stand close to him. They were at the back of the space, now, both seeming to lean forward into the towering white curtain, almost pressing their ears against it. Briefly, it occurred to me to wonder where the blond kids had gone. Fifteen feet or so to my left, the attendant shifted, stared at me, and the change dispenser rattled against his waist. I started forward, got within five steps of my wife and my oldest friend, and became aware, at last, of the new sounds.

Actually, the sounds had been there all along, I think. I'd just assumed that the murmuring was coming from the ocean, the bursts of rhythmic clatter from the arcade machines. But they originated on the other side of this curtain. For the second time, I thought of the Wizard of Oz in his cubicle, furiously pulling levers to make the world magical and terrible. More magical and terrible than tornadoes and red shoes in green grass and dead or disappearing loved ones and home had already made it.

Ash glanced over his shoulder at me. I stepped forward, uncertainly, and stood behind him. Reaching out slowly, he brushed the curtain with his fingers, causing barely a stir in the heavy material.

"Crawl under?" he muttered. "Just push through?"

He bent to lift the curtain's skirt, and my wife turned briefly toward me, so that I caught just a glimpse of her face. Her lips had gone completely flat, and all trace of color had leached out of her cheeks.

"You know what's back there, don't you?" I said, as the attendant rattled closer, and Ash disappeared under the curtain.

"It's why we're here," said my wife, and followed him.

What struck me first as I struggled through the curtain and shrugged it off was the motion. Even before I made sense of what I was seeing, the whole space seemed to tilt, as though we'd stepped onto some sort of colorful, rotating platform. The color came courtesy of a red neon sign that hissed and spat blue sparks into the air. The sign was nailed to a wooden pillar that had been driven through the planking of the pier right beside where we emerged. I didn't even process what it said for a few seconds, and when I did, the words meant nothing to me, anyway. *LITE YOUR LINE LITE YOURS...*

"Change?" murmured a voice, right in front of me, and I jerked back farther still, bumping against the curtain and feelings its weight on my back.

The girl who'd spoken couldn't have been out of her teens.

Her skin glowed translucent red in the tinted neon like sea glass. Her eyes were brown and bright, her lips full but colorless and expressionless. Her brown hair swept up off her scalp and arced in a slow inward curl to her shoulders, but where it brushed her black turtleneck, the tips had turned white, like a breaking wave upside down.

Before I could say anything, she was floating away, the smoothness of her movements terrifying until I realized she was on roller skates. Her wheels made bumping sounds between the planks.

"Hi, Dad," Rebecca whispered, shoulders rigid, arms tucked tight to her sides, and my eyes flew around the space.

Mostly, what I saw were machines. Ten stubby, silver pinball tables jammed together end to end at awkward, irregular angles like dodge-'em cars between rides. Hunched in identical poses over the glass tabletops were the players, and none of them looked up. They just kept pulling what I assumed were the ball-release levers and then pushing and patting at the flipper controls on the sides. Straight across the space from us, his ass to the drapery that hung from the magician's hat and divided this space from the night and the open ocean, a fifty-ish, red-haired guy with tufts of wiry beard sprouting from the cracks in his craggy face like weeds through pavement, bent almost perpendicular over his machine, whispering to it as his fingers pummeled the buttons. I could just see the ripped, faded American flag design on his T-shirt when he rocked back to jack another ball into play.

"Oh my God, Rebecca. That isn't—"

"Huh?" she said, still rigid.

Of course it wasn't really her father, I realized. I'd seen pictures. And anyway, she wasn't looking at the red-headed man, or any of the other players. She was watching the electric board that hung, like the *LITE YOUR LINE LITE YOURS* sign, on another wooden pillar across the space from us. It was flashing the numbers *012839*. Every few seconds, the numbers blinked.

Abruptly, a bell dinged, and the display on the electric board changed. #5, it read now. And then, *Congratulations! You're Liter!* Then bumping sounds as the roller-skate girl swept the room, removing quarters from atop each player's machine, and dropping a single red poker chip at the feet of the red-haired man.

"Change?" she said to us, gliding past without looking or stopping, and abruptly Ash was out amongst them, assuming a place at a table kitty-corner to the American flag man's. On the board, a new number flashed. *081034.* The lever-jerking and button-tapping resumed in earnest. American flag man never looked up.

I watched Ash glance at the numbers board, down into his machine, across to American flag man. Then he was pulling his own lever, nodding. There were now five players: two stick-thin older women in matching bright red poodle skirts, twin sets, and bobby socks, who might have been sisters; a kid in skater shorts with some kind of heavy metal music erupting from the sides of his headphones, as though everything inside his skull were kicking and screaming to get out of there; American flag man; and Ash.

"What planet is this?" I murmured, and a bell dinged, and the roller-skate girl circled the room once more while Ash rocked back and laughed and dropped another quarter on top of his machine for the girl to collect.

Closing her eyes, Rebecca surprised me by taking my hand. Then she leaned in and kissed my cheek. "This is where he came. Before he walked out. It's been just like this for…God." She shuddered. "He'd put us on the merry-go-round, and he'd come in here, and he'd spend his hours. One quarter at a time. Most days, he wouldn't even take us home. My mom had to come get us."

Another ding, and the kid in the skater shorts flipped his hands in the air and moonwalked a few steps to his right, then back to his machine to pop a quarter in place just as the roller-skate girl passed and dropped a red chip at his feet. One of the women in the poodle skirts laughed. The laugh sounded gentler than I expected. The board flashed, and a new round began.

"Ever played?" I said, holding my wife's hand, but not too tight. Around us, the canvas outer draping undulated in slow motion as the sea breeze pushed against and through it. There was another winner, another burst of quiet laughter from somewhere as some lucky soul got *Liter*, another new number flashing. One more sad-magic night with Ash and Rebecca, so long after the last one that I'd forgotten how it felt.

A good while after I'd asked, Rebecca sighed and leaned her head against me. "I miss our daughter," she said.

"Me, too."

"Should we call?"

"She's alright."

"Look at him," Rebecca said, and we did, together.

He was bent almost as far over his machine as the red-headed man, now, and when he played, the lights inside it and the red neon from the *LITE YOURS* sign reflected off his skull, and his vest beat and twitched with the rhythm of his movements, as though we were looking straight through his skin at the mechanisms that ran him.

"Poor Ash," I murmured, though I wasn't sure why I felt that way, and suspected he'd be furious if he heard me say it.

"I'll bet you a bag of Patriot Popcorn I can win before he does," said Rebecca, and she straightened and let go of my hand.

I thought of the fisherman on the empty pier behind us with the ray dying in his lap, the gaggle of beggars, and beyond them, the brightly lit streets of downtown Long Beach. "And where will we find Patriot Popcorn, wife of mine, now that the Gap has come?"

"I think I know a place."

"I bet you do," I said. On every side of us, at all times, at least one person was laughing.

"Change?" said the roller-skate girl, gliding past, but she executed a perfect stop even before Rebecca got her hand to her pocket. She took my wife's dollar, nodded. Her turtleneck clung tight to her, and there were tiny beads of sweat along the mouth of it like a string of transparent pearls. The tingle that sizzled through me then was more charged than any I'd felt since adolescence but sadder and therefore sexier still, and I had to bend over until it passed. Whether it was for my wife, the roller-skate girl, or just the evening, I had no idea.

When I next looked up, Rebecca and Ash were side by side, both bent over their individual metal machines, fingers pushing and pumping while the lights on the metal board flashed and the roller-skate girl rolled and the ocean breathed, in and out. Not wanting to distract them—and also, for some reason, not wanting to play—I stepped just close enough to see how the game worked.

Inside each machine was a ball chute and a simple, inclined wooden playing board, with metallic mushrooms sprouting out of the center and impeding or—if you were skilled enough—directing the path of the ball. Across the top of the playing board were ball-sized holes numbered one to ten in plain black lettering. The object was to sink one ball in each of the holes corresponding with the flashing numbers on the big board. When you dropped a ball in the correct hole, your machine dinged and the number lit up. First person to light up every required number got a visit from the roller-skate girl and a red chip dropped at his or her feet as the quarter antes were collected for the next round. Then, with no pause, no stretch-break, no breath, the big board flashed again and the game resumed.

I settled into my spot between Rebecca and Ash, close enough to touch both but a step back. I was watching my wife's frame rattle as she bounced up and down in her big black shoes, leaned left and then right, and I thought of the new, permanently puffy space on her stomach where her scar was, and where, she said, she could no longer feel anything, which for some reason always made me want to put my hand there. I watched her watch Ash between games, heard her gleeful, competitive murmurs.

"Feel that, Ash? That would be my breath on your neck. That's me passing you by. Again."

Ash kept shaking his head, staring into his machine and seeming to drag it closer to him with those outsized, outstretched arms. "Not this time," he kept saying. "Not tonight."

And I found that I knew—that I'd always known—that Rebecca was in love with him, too. That I was merely the post she and Ash circled, eyeing one another from either side of me but never getting closer than they already were. The knowledge felt strange, heavy in my chest, horrible but also old. As though I hadn't discovered but remembered it. Also, I knew she loved me, in the permanent way she'd loved her mother, whom she'd stayed with, after all. Not that she'd had a choice.

In the back, the man in the flag shirt lit his line, closed his eyes, and slapped the sides of his machine with the heels of his palms. Then the kid in the headphones won again, did his dance. Occasionally, one of the poodle-skirt women won, but mostly they didn't, and their laughs punctuated each round, regardless. Rebecca bobbed, swore, taunted Ash. Ash leaned over farther, grim-faced, muttering, the machine bumping and dinging against him, almost attached to him now like an iron lung. Between and amongst them, the roller-skate girl skated, collecting quarters, strewing victory chips. At one point, tears developed in my eyes, and I wiped them away fast and thought of the perpetual sprinkles of dried milk that dotted the corners of my daughter's lips like fairy dust. The stuff that brought her life.

It was the poker chips, I think, that finally alerted me to how long we'd been standing there. My eyes kept following the roller-skate girl on her sweeps, tracing her long fingers on their circumscribed, perfectly circular path from machine-top to black change-purse at her waist, white tips of her hair barely caressing the slope of her shoulders. And at last my gaze followed one of those chips as it fell to the floor amidst maybe a thousand others strewn around the ankles of the flag-shirt man like rose petals after a rainstorm.

My head jerked as though I'd been slapped.

"Change?" the roller-skate girl said as she breezed past me on her path through the players. Had she said that to me ever▪

time? Had I answered? And where was the music coming from? I could hear it faintly. I was moving to it, a little. So was Ash. A gently bouncing fairground whirl, from an organ somewhere not too near. Under the dock? On shore?

Inside me? Because I appeared to be singing it. Sort of. Breathing it, so it was barely audible. We all were, I thought. It was everywhere, floating in the air of this makeshift room like a sea breeze trapped when the curtains dropped. Dazed, I watched Rebecca fish ten dollars out of her jeans pocket without looking up. The roller-skate girl took it and stood a bankroll of quarters, wrapped tight in red paper like a stick of dynamite, on the rim of Rebecca's machine. Both of them humming.

"Rebecca?" I said, then said it again, because my voice sounded funny, slurred and slow, as though I were speaking under water.

"Just a sec," she told me.

"Rebecca, come on."

"Might as well," Ash murmured. "I'm almost there. No hope for you."

My wife glanced up—slowly, smoothly—and caught my eye. "Hear that? You'd think he'd beaten me all his life. Or ever. At anything."

"I think we should go," I said, as Rebecca's head sank down over the metal tabletop again and her hands drifted to the ball-lever and buttons. I said it again, and my words got tangled up in that tune. I was almost singing them, and then I smashed my jaws together so hard I felt my two top front teeth pop in their sockets. "*Rebecca*," I snapped.

And just like that, as though I'd doused her with ice water, my wife shivered upright. Shudders rippled all the way down her body. Her skin seemed to have come loose. I could almost see it billowing around her. Then she was weeping. "Fuck him, Elliot," she said. "Oh, fuck him *so fucking much. God,* I miss my mom."

For one moment more, I stood paralyzed, this time by the sight of my weeping wife, though I could feel that tune bubbling up again in the back of my mouth, as though my insides were boiling, threatening to stream out of me like steam. Finally, Rebecca's fingers found mine. They felt reassuringly bony and hard. Familiar.

"Let's go," she whispered, still weeping.

"Come on come on come on *Yah!*" Ash screeched, started to hurl his arms over his head and stopped, scowling as the board flashed the number of the winner and the American flag man closed his eyes and popped the sides of his machine with his palms once more. "I had it," said Ash, already hunching forward. "I really thought I had it."

"Time to go, bud," I told him, pushing my fingers against Rebecca's so both of us could feel the joints grinding together. She was still shuddering, head down, and the roller-skate girl glided up and swept a new quarter from Ash's machine and reached for the top one on Rebecca's stack and Rebecca swatted the whole roll to the floor. The roller-skate girl didn't look up or stop humming as she passed.

"Right now," Rebecca said, looking up, letting the tears stream down. "It's got to be now, Elliot."

"Come on, Ash," I said. "Let's go get *tapas.*"

"What are you talking about?" he said, and the big board flashed, and he was playing again. The kid in the headphones won in a matter of seconds.

"Ash. We need to leave."

"Almost there," he said. "Don't you want to see what you win?"

"Elliot," Rebecca said, voice tight, fingers like talons ripping at my wrist.

"Ash, come—"

"Elliot. *Run.* " She was staring up into the magician's hat, then at the American flag man, who didn't stare back, hadn't ever seemed to notice we were there.

Another number on the board, another flurry of fingers and rattle of pinballs, another burst of laughter from the women in poodle skirts. Then we were gone, Rebecca yanking me behind her like a puppy on a leash. Low humming sounds streamed from our mouths as we struggled through the white curtain and just kept going.

"Hey," I said, trying to shake her fingers just a little looser on my arm, but she didn't let go until we were through the outer canvas, standing in the biting air on the wet and rotting dock. Instantly, the tune was gone from my mouth and ears, as though someone had snapped shut the lid of a music box. I found myself trying to remember it, and was seized, suddenly, by a grief so all-engulfing I could barely breathe, and didn't want to. Tears exploded onto my cheeks.

Rebecca stirred, let go of my arm, but turned to me. "Oh," she said, reached up, stuck her finger in one of my teardrops and traced it all over my cheek, as though finger-painting with it.

"I don't know why," I said, and I didn't. But it had nothing to do with Ash, or Ash and Rebecca, or Rebecca's dead mother, or our strange, loving, incomplete marriage. It had to do with our daughter. So new to the world.

"Come on," she said.

"What about our friend in there?"

"He'll follow."

"What if he doesn't?"

"He knows where we live. He's a big boy."

"Rebecca," I said, but realized I didn't know what I was going to say. What came out was, "I don't know. There's something…"

Around us, the sea stirred, began to slap against the shore and the pilings beneath it. We could feel it through our feet. The reassuring beat of the blood of the earth. There was a mist now, too, and it left little wet spots on our exposed skin.

Rebecca shrugged. "It's just where my dad is. Where he'll always be. For me."

Then we were walking. Again, our footsteps sounded strange, made almost no sound whatsoever. There was still no moon overhead, only gray-white clouds, lit from behind from millions of miles away. The fishermen had remained in their places, but they'd gone almost motionless, leaning over their lines into the night as though every single one of them had gone to sleep. I saw the guy who'd caught the ray, but the ray was no longer in his lap, and I wondered what he'd done with it. Looking up, I saw the blacked-out buildings of old Long Beach, seemingly farther from us than they should have been, wrapped in mist and scaffolding like mothballed furniture in an attic. By the time we reached our car, the feeling in my chest had eased a bit, and I was no longer crying and still couldn't figure out why I had been. Rebecca was shivering again.

"Let's wait here for him," I said, and Rebecca shivered harder.

"No."

She got in the car, and I climbed in beside her. I turned on the ignition but waited a while. When Rebecca looked at me next, she was wearing the expression I'd become so familiar with during this last, long, sweet year. Eyes still bright, but dazed somehow. Mouth pursed, but softly. "Take me home to see my girl," she said.

I didn't argue. I stopped thinking about Ash. I took my wife home to our tiny house.

That was Friday. Saturday we stayed in our neighborhood, took strolls with our child, went to bed very early and touched each other a while without making love. Sunday I got up and made eggs and wondered where Ash had gone and whether he was angry with us, and then we went hiking up the fire trail behind our subdivision into the hills, brown and strangled with drought. I didn't worry, really. But I started calling Ash's Oakland bungalow on Monday morning. I also called the hospital where he worked, and on Thursday, right when he'd apparently told Ms. Paste he would return, he turned up as scheduled for his shift on the ward. I got him on the line, and he said he had rounds to do and would call me back. He didn't, though. Then, or ever.

After that, I stopped thinking about him for a while. It wasn't unusual for Ash to disappear from our lives for months or even years on end. I already understood that adult friendships operated differently from high school or college ones, were harbors to visit rather than places to live, no matter how sweet and safe the harbor. Rebecca never mentioned him. Our baby learned to walk. The next time I called the hospital, maybe six months ago, I was told Ash no longer worked there.

Last night, late, I climbed out of my bed, looked at my daughter lying sideways, arms akimbo, across the head of her crib mattress like a game piece that had popped free of its box slot and rolled loose, and wandered into the living room to read the newspaper. I opened the *Calendar* section, stared at the photograph on the second page. My mouth went dry, as though every trace of saliva had been sucked from it, and my bones locked in place. I couldn't move, couldn't breathe, couldn't even think.

Staring out at me was a photograph of a merry-go-round horse, tipped sideways as it was hauled out of storage by movers. Its front teeth were chipped and aimed in opposing directions below the oversized, grinning lips, and its lifted hooves seemed to be scrambling frantically at the air.

Last Rooff horses sold at auction, read the caption.

I flew through the story that accompanied the photograph, processing it in bits and pieces, while fragments of that tune—the one from the pier—floated free in my head but never knitted themselves into something I could hum.

> Once, these vibrantly painted, joyous creatures spun and flew on the soon-to-be-razed Long Beach Pier...The last great work of a grieving man...His final carousel, populated with what Rooff called "the company I crave" after his longtime business partner and reputed lover, Los Angeles nightclub owner and legendary gambler Daniel R. Ratch, took his own life following a decades-long battle with a degenerative muscular disease in September of 1898.
>
> The reclusive Rooff and notorious Ratch formed one of the more unlikely—and lucrative—financial partnerships of the fin-de-siecle era, building thousands of cheaply manufactured

carousels, fortune-telling machines, and other amusements of the time for boardwalks and parks nationwide. They envisioned the Long Beach Pier as their crowning achievement, a world unto itself for "all the laughing people...," in Rooff's memorable phrase at his tearful press conference following Ratch's death...

Rooff completed only the carousel and the now infamous Lite-Your-Line parlor before being fired for erratic behavior and the agonizingly slow pace of his work... He disappeared from the public record, and his death is not recorded.

There was more, but the words had stopped making sense to me. Shoving the paper away, I sat back in my chair. The trembling started a few seconds later.

I can't explain how I knew. I was thinking of Rooff under that hat, hidden by curtains, working furiously in the candlelight, chanting his dead lover's name. I think maybe I'd always suspected, hadn't admitted. But Ash had made it back to Oakland, hadn't he? And we'd made it here?

Then, abruptly, I was up, snatching my keys off the hook next to the kitchen sink and fleeing toward our car while that incomplete tune whirled in my head and the whole last night with Ash spilled in front of my eyes in kaleidoscopic broken pieces. I don't remember a single second of the drive down the freeways, couldn't even tell you whether there was traffic, because all I was seeing were the homeless men and the sores on their arms and the way their mouths moved as they chanted their rhyme. Then I was seeing the ray flapping in midair, lifted out of the waves just as we passed, as though the whole scene had been triggered by our passing. The disappearing blond children, the arcade machine attendant's graceful shuffle and the sound he made. The rose-petal poker chips. The tinkling machines. The glide of the roller-skate girl, and the skater kid's moonwalk, and the American flag man. And the poodle-skirt women's perpetually smiling faces. Most of all, their faces, and it was their laughter I was hearing as I skidded into that giant, empty parking lot and jammed my car to a stop and leapt out, hoping, praying.

Even the streetlights were gone, and the dark pier jutted crookedly over the quietly lapping water like the prow of a beached ship. No magician's hat. Nothing on the pier at all. Overhead, I saw stars, faint and smeared by the smog, as though I were viewing them through a greasy window. Behind me, the new old city, safely shut down and swept clean for the night, rocked imperceptibly on its foundations. A wind kicked up, freezing cold, and I clamped my arms to my chest and crouched beside my car and wished I'd remembered a jacket, at least.

Finally, I let myself think it. Sort what I'd been hoping. Which had been what, exactly? That I'd find the auctioneer still here? That the movers would still be emptying the last pieces out of the warehouse, and maybe I could...

"What?" I said aloud, and slammed my palms against the pavement and scraped them badly. *Do what?* Pick up my friend's body like a cigar store Indian, tie him to the top of the car, bring him to our house, which he'd never seen, and prop him on our little porch in our choice of vests? Maybe bring along a poodle-skirt woman so we could make set pieces?

Staggering to my feet, I took a huge breath and let the ocean air cut my lungs. In my pocket, I realized, I'd crumpled the newspaper article, and I removed it now, opened it, ripped it to pieces, and set the pieces flying. Rebecca could never see that article, could never know what I was thinking. It was bad enough—it was flat, fucking murder—that we'd left Ash down here. I didn't even want to imagine how she'd react when she realized what really might have happened to her father.

How did it work, I wondered? Were Rooff's ghosts, or machines, or whatever they were, *selective* about the company they brought him? Had they let us go, or had we refused? Had Ash known, before it was too late, that he had a choice? Had the rest of them—the roller-skate girl, the flag man, the kid, maybe even Rebecca's father—chosen to stay, because it was bright and musical and happy in there, and smelled of the sea?

It was almost light when I fumbled my car door open and collapsed back into the driver's seat. I could be wrong, I thought. I could go home right now and find Rebecca with the kitchen phone dangling from her ear, smiling in the way she didn't anymore as Ash told her where he'd vanished to this time and she spooned minced carrots to our child. But I didn't think so.

Not until I was off the freeways again, just pulling into our little driveway, did it occur to me to wonder where, exactly, Rooff's last merry-go-round stopped. At the edge of the white curtain? Or the end of the pier? The ray could have been part of it, and the fishermen, and the beggars, too. Or maybe they'd just wanted to be.

I stepped out of the car, felt the stagnant L.A. air settle around me. The rising sun caught in my neighbor's windows, releasing tiny prisms of colored light, and somewhere down the street, wind chimes clinked, though there was little wind. And the feeling that whispered through me then was indeed magical, terrible, and also almost sweet. Because I realized I might be underestimating the power of Rooff's last carousel, even now. We could be on it, still—Rebecca, me, the whole crazy, homogenizing coast—bobbing up and down in our prescribed places as our parents die and our friends whirl past and away again and the places we love evaporate out of the world, the way everyone's favorite people and places inevitably do. Until, finally, we are just our faces, smiles frozen bright as we can make them, hands stretching for our children because we can't help but hope they'll join us, hope they'll understand before we did that there really may be no place else to go or at least forgive us for not finding it. Then they'll smile back at us. Climb aboard. And ride.

Safety Clowns

"*and*

the

goat-footed

baloonMan   *whistles*

far
and
wee"
—e.e. cummings

As soon as I spotted the ad, I knew I'd found what I wanted.

Like being the Good Guy? Like happy faces? Safe driver? Safety Clown needs you.

One phone call and thirty seconds later, I had an interview appointment for 5:45 the following morning with Jaybo, dispatcher, founder, and managing owner of the Safety Clown Ice Cream Truck Company. "Bring your license," Jaybo half-shouted at me, voice hoarse as a carnival barker's, and hung up.

Replacing the phone, I lifted the red dry-erase marker out of its clip on the message board and made a tentative check next to item #7 on my mom's list: *Find USEFUL summer employment. Help people. Have stories to tell. Make enough to concentrate on school in the fall.* Then I sat down on the tiny lanai to watch the evening marine layer of fog roll in off the beach and fill the ravine between our condo complex and the horse racing track down the hill.

My condo complex. I still couldn't get used to it.

My mother had scrawled her final message board list for me in the middle of the night, three hours before I drove her to the hospice to die. That had been a little over a month ago, orphaning me on the eve of my twentieth birthday. She'd left me our one-and-a-half bedroom condo, enough cash to finish my sophomore year at San Diego State without taking any new loans or other job beyond my work-study at the library, and her cactus garden. "No way even you can kill those," she'd told me, touching her fingers one final time to the tiny prickles in each individual window box. It had taken me less than four weeks to prove her wrong.

The morning of my interview, I set the alarm for 4:45 but woke a little after three, prickly and unable to sleep any more. After this, the only undone item on her list would be #1: *Celebrate your birthday.* And it was a little late for that. So. No more mom lists. Nothing left to do for anyone but me. Already, I was certain I'd sell this place, maybe before September. And I'd slowly lose the memory of air-conditioners hissing in all the condos jammed up against ours. I'd forget 4:15 a.m. garbage trucks and dogs snarling through screen doors at the hot-air balloons climbing with the light to lift rich people into the sunrise.

But I probably wouldn't forget the summer afternoons playing skateboard tag with the thousand other kid residents in the alleys of our sprawling nowhere of town-home blocks, stealing each other's wish-pennies out of the fountain by the guard shack, and waiting for 3:30, when the ice cream trucks descended en masse and we engulfed them. Hours after the trucks left, the buzzing tinkle of their music stayed trapped in our ears, like the bubble of pool water you can't quite shake out.

Getting this job would be my farewell, not just fulfillment of my mother's wishes but tribute to her. To my father, too, although what I mostly remembered about him was the smell of the strawberry air-freshener he insisted my mother spray all around to hide his sick smell, even though it didn't, and the way he'd died, holding his wife's and his seven-year-old son's hands in his surprisingly strong ones, croaking, "God. Damn. I can feel myself going down."

At breakfast, alone in my condo, I watched the marine layer through the open lanai door, hearing horses nickering as stable-hands led them to the beach. Right on time, I left, pointing my mother's battered blue Geo down the empty I-5 freeway. I kept the window down, and the fog buffeted my face as though I were piloting a speedboat. Jaybo's directions pointed me above 10th Street into a motionless neighborhood of empty lots and warehouses. At that hour, even uphill and inland, mist streamed from the lampposts and chain link fences. Reaching C Street, I slowed, turned, and began creeping east, looking for a street number or sign. What I saw, mostly, were human-shaped humps curled under newspapers or garbage bags along the fencing. I was about to turn around when I spotted the hand-lettered poster board lashed by its corners to a post at the end of an other-wise deserted block:

SAFETY CLOWN.

Next to the letters, someone had drawn a primitive yellow sun, with pathetic first-grade rays pointing in too many direc-tions, so that it looked more like a beetle. I parked, walked along the fence until I located an opening, and stepped through it.

I got maybe five steps into the lot before I stopped. Strands of fog brushed against my face and hands like a spider web I'd walked through. My shoulders crept up, my hands curled in my pockets, and I stood rooted, listening. Peering to my left, I confronted the dead headlights of five hulking white vans. I looked right and found five more vans facing me in a perfect line. No movement, no lights, no people anywhere.

I was in a parking lot, after all. Discovering actual vehicles parked there rated fairly low on the discomforting revelations scale. Except for what was sprouting from them.

Clinging to them?

I took a step back, realized that put me closer to the vans behind me, and checked them, too. Sure enough, giant cockroach-shaped shadows clung vertically to each sliding passenger door from top to bottom, spindle-legs folded under-neath and laced through the handles, tiny heads jutting from between knobby, jointed shoulders. It was the fog—only the fog—that made them twitch, as though preparing to lift into the air like locusts.

"Hey Jaybo," a voice called, surprisingly close behind me, and I turned again. From somewhere among the left-hand vans, a man had emerged. He had red hair, dark coveralls, a grease rag sliding around and between his fingers like a snake he was cradling.

The barker's voice I'd heard on the phone yesterday answered him. "Yep?"

"Think our lucky newbie's here."

"What's he look like?"

The guy in the coveralls flipped his grease rag onto his shoulder and stared me up and down. "Kind of short. Too thin, like maybe he needs some ice cream. Good bones. I like him."

A door clicked open toward the back of the lot, and another face peered out. This one was narrow, with bulbous green eyes and a mouth that hung a little open even at rest, like an eel's. "Come on in," Jaybo said, and retreated into the lighted space.

Why did I have to be here this early, anyway?

The manager's office proved to be a silver Airstream trailer lodged against the wall of a warehouse. Making my way there, I sensed shapes drifting behind windshields, cockroach shadows shivering as the vans rocked and the fog swept over them, and with a flash of disappointment I realized that these had to be the ice cream trucks. I'd been hoping for the milkman-style vehicles that used to service us, with their bright blue stickers of Popsicle Rockets and Igloo Pies pasted unevenly all over the sides like Garbage Pail Kid stickers on a lunchbox. I wondered if these vans even played music.

Hand extended, I stepped into the trailer. "Good morning, Mr. Jaybo, I'm Max Wa—"

"Just Jaybo. You're not that short."

Instead of accepting my offered shake, he waved one arm in the air between us. The arm had no hand on the end, or at least no fingers, ending in a bulging ball of red skin. I dropped my own hand awkwardly to my side.

"Thin, though." He cocked his head. Up close, his eyes were almost yellow behind his filthy round glasses. Stubby silver hair studded his skull like pins in a cushion. "Think you're going to love all kinds of things about this job."

Except for a small stack of ledger paper and a pen cup full of cheap, chewed-on Bics, Jaybo's desk had nothing on it. On the wall behind him, he'd tacked a massive map of San Diego County, with snaky pink and blue lines crisscrossing it like veins. Other than the map and a green, steel file cabinet, the trailer's only adornment was an Al Italia calendar, two years out of date, opened to April and featuring a photograph of a woman with astonishingly long, silky brunette hair and a smooth-fitting stewardess uniform, smiling sweetly. The caption read, *Roma? Perfect.*

"You're Italian?" I asked as Jaybo settled behind the desk and dropped both his hand and his stump across it. There was nowhere for me to sit.

"If she is," he said, smiled with his mouth still dangling open, and wiggled the fingers he had at me. "License."

I gave mine to him. He noted the details on his ledger. Remembering this was an interview—the whole morning had felt more like sleepwalking—I straightened, smoothing my checked shirt where it disappeared into the waist of my khakis.

"Like kids, Maxwell?"

"Always. Last summer I—"

"Like making people's days better? Giving them something to look forward to?"

"Sure."

"You're hired. You'll train today with Randy. *Randy!*"

I shuffled in place. "That's it?"

Jaybo turned slightly in his chair and winked, either at me or his Al Italia woman. "I know trustworthy people when I meet them. And anyway." He grinned, thumping his stump on the desktop. "You're going to love this job."

The door of the Airstream burst open, and I turned to find the entry completely blotted out, as though some massive, magic beanstalk had sprouted there in the three minutes I'd been inside. The beanstalk bent forward, and an ordinary head popped under the top of the doorframe.

"Randy," said Jaybo. "This is Max. Make him one of us."

Randy had neatly cropped brown hair with a few shoots of gray along the temples, slitty brown eyes, and a jaw so long I half-expected him to whinny. Inviting me out by inclining his head, Randy withdrew, revealing the foggy world once more as he stood to his full height.

He wasn't that big, out in the air. My head nearly reached his shoulders, which looked square and hard under a tight green camouflage T. So maybe 6'5"? 6'7"? If he stood with his legs together, I thought I could probably get my arms around his calves. Maybe even his knees.

Wordlessly, he led me around back of the trailer toward the long cement warehouse that formed the property's northern-most boundary. He whistled quietly but expertly as he did so, with little trills and grace notes. After a few seconds, the tune registered, and I started laughing.

Randy swung that epic jaw toward me. "Join in. I know you know it." His voice had an odd, strangled quality, as if his throat were too narrow for the rest of him, like the barrel of a bassoon.

I did as he'd directed. *"She'll be coming 'round the mountain when she comes."* Maybe the vans played music after all.

The warehouse door was metal and ribbed and freshly painted white. Still whistling, Randy beat on it with the heel of one huge hand, and it shuddered like a gong.

"C'mon, Monkey, open up, we got joy to spread." The jaw swung my way again like the boom of a sailboat. "Randy, by the way."

"I'm Max."

"IMAX. Big Screen."

I had no idea whether that was a non sequitur or a nickname, but it made me laugh again. Randy pummeled the door some more, and it jerked and lifted off the ground on its chain. Freezing air spilled over our feet.

"Freezer," I announced, instantly felt stupid, and so employed Mom's Law of Idiotic Comments: go one stupider. "For the ice cream."

"Big Screen," Randy said, and thumped me on the shoulder.

Inside, I found myself facing a desk made from a slab of wood and twenty or so stacked milk crates. This desk was as empty as Jaybo's except for a sleek black ThinkPad folded open. Behind the desk on a swivel chair sat the grease-rag guy who'd greeted me, wearing gloves now. Beyond him, ceiling-high stacks of cardboard boxes with clear stretch-plastic tops fell away in rows to the back of the warehouse and out to both side walls.

"How many, Randy-man?" said the guy at the desk. His rag lolled from the pocket of his work-shirt like a friendly, panting tongue.

"Feeling good today, Monkey. Thinking Big Screen here's going to bring me luck. Let's go twenty and twenty."

Monkey shook his head and tapped the tab key on his keyboard. "Going to put us all to shame. You're learning from the best, kid. All-time champ."

Resuming his whistling, Randy marched past the desk, tousling Monkey's hair. At the first stack, Randy hunched, got his arms around the bottom box, and held there like a weightlifter preparing for a clean-and-jerk. Then he just stood up, no effort at all, and the boxes came off the ground and towered in his arms.

"God*damn*, Randy," said a new voice from the entry, and I turned to find three new people lined up by Monkey's desk. The speaker had to be over seventy, long and thinner than I was in his gray denim jacket and red Urban Outfitters cap. Next to him stood a Chinese kid about my age, and behind them a yellow-haired forty-something woman in sneakers and a sundress.

"Morning, slow pokes," Randy said, pointing toward another stack with his foot. "Big Screen, grab me another five, would you, and bring them out front?"

"Must eat half of it himself," the old guy muttered.

"He doesn't touch ice cream and you know it," said the woman in the sundress, and Randy nudged her affectionately with his elbow as he strode past.

Under cover of the patter, I approached the nearest stack of boxes, slid my arms around the top five, and gasped. They were freezing. As soon as I lifted them, the crooks of my elbows began to ache, and my fingers cramped. But at least they were lighter than I was expecting. I gazed through the clear plastic of the topmost box. There they were, in their garish orange and Kool Aid-red wrappers. *We'll be bringing Popsicle Rockets when we come…*

"Hey, Randy," Monkey called as the big man reached the door. When Randy turned, Monkey tossed him a long white envelope, overstuffed and rubber-banded twice around. Without any sort of hitch or arm adjustment, Randy stretched out his fingers and snatched the envelope out of the air, pressing it against his tower of boxes. "Might want to count that."

The sound Randy made came as close to *pshaw* as anything I've heard an actual human attempt. He strode into the fog, and I hurried after him.

"See, Big Screen," he said without turning around, "we're all independent contractors. Great system. You pay for your product up front, in full, so the trick is buying only what you're going to sell. Jaybo gets thirty percent, Monkey gets five for keeping your van running smooth, and that's it. Rest is yours, in cash, free and clear."

Even after he mentioned the vans, I somehow forgot about the cockroach things until we were halfway to the front of the lot. The cold and the weight from the boxes seemed to have latched onto my ribs like pincers. When I remembered and looked up, the figures were where I'd left them, just hanging against the van doors the way spiders do when you stare at them.

Randy went right on talking. "But see, the best thing about Sunshine Safety Clown, Jaybo's got the routes laid out for you. Long a route as you want, street by street, stop by stop. These are guaranteed sales, man. *Guaranteed.* You saw Jaybo's map?"

"And his girl," I murmured, boxes starting to slip, eyes still flitting between vans.

"What girl?" Randy lowered into a squat and settled his boxes on the asphalt next to the front-most right-hand van.

"Guess we have different priorities." I lowered my own boxes a little too fast. The bottom one thumped.

"Careful, Big Screen. You bought those, you know. Alright, I'll open her up and let's feed her."

Did I imagine him pausing for just a moment as he approached the van's side? His fingers drummed the thighs of his jeans, and his whistling ceased. Then he jammed his hand between those giant, spindly legs, twisted sideways as though tearing out a heart, and ripped open the van door.

He came back fast, whistling, and hoisted the top five boxes off his stack.

"Randy, what is that?"

"What?" he said.

"On the side of the van."

"He's...a friend. Load up, and I'll show you."

For the next fifteen minutes, we arranged ice cream cases in the freezer bins that lined the inside walls of the back of the van. Around us, meanwhile, activity increased throughout the lot as more doors slid open and more ice cream disappeared into bins. Randy worked quickly. When we'd finished, he banged the bin lids shut and hopped out fast and started around front.

"Close that door, will you?" he called over his shoulder.

If there'd been a way up front from where I was, I'd have used the inside handle. But the back of the van had been sealed off, probably to help maintain coolness, and so I had no choice but to hop down and face the bug thing.

Up close, it looked wooden. The fog had left a wet residue on its slats, and I could see splotches of colored paint all up and down them. I remembered my mom taking me to the natural history museum in Balboa Park once to see newborn moths dangling from their burst cocoons, wings drying.

Randy stuck his head out the passenger window. "Hurry up. Don't let the heat in."

With a grunt I didn't realize was coming, I reached into the nest of slats, grasped the metal handle at their center, and yanked. The door leapt onto its runners and closed with a click.

"Okay. Back up," Randy said. "Farther."

I could see him at the wheel, hand poised over the control panel. "Say hello," he said, and pulled down hard.

For a second, the bug thing quivered on the pegs holding it to the van. Then it unfolded. First a leg, human-shaped, popped free of the nest and dropped earthward as though feeling for the ground. As soon as that one was fully extended, another fell. The legs had purple striping, as did the arms, which clicked open, pointing sideways. Finally, the head sprang up, tiny black eyes staring at me above a deflated balloon nose, wide red happy mouth.

Thinking that was it, I peeled myself off the neighboring van where I'd been watching. Then the whole clown pivoted on its pegs and swung perpendicular to Randy's door. Its puffy marsh-mallow of a right hand pointed its little red STOP sign right at my heart.

I stepped around it to the passenger-side window. "That's for cars, right? So kids can cross the street?"

Randy nodded.

I grinned. "It'd work on me."

"Me, too."

"Jaybo made those?"

Randy shook his head. "Loubob." When he saw my expression, he cocked his head in surprise. "You know Loubob?"

Memory poured through me, of my father with his determined, trembling hands on the steering wheel as he drove us to Loubobland the night before Halloween, two months before he died. The last time I'd been in a car with him.

"Yeah," I said. "I mean, I've been there. The muffler men."

"The muffler men," said Randy, and nodded. "Hop up."

I did, remembering that long, silent drive east into the

farmlands of Fallbrook, the sun pumping redness over the horizon as it sank behind us. I couldn't recall a single thing my father and I had said to each other. But I could still see Loubob's junkyard. He'd been a carnival skywheel technician, the story went, then a funhouse specialist, then a circus-truck mechanic before retiring to sell off a career's worth of accumulated spare parts and create annual Halloween displays out of rusted mufflers and scrap metal and hand-built motors. His muffler men wrapped themselves around eucalyptus tree trunks as though trying to shinny up them, shambled from behind junk piles like prowling silver skeletons, dangled from overhead branches to bump shoulders with shrieking guests. My father had loved it.

When I'd buckled myself in, Randy released the lever on the control panel, and the Safety Clown clattered back into place against the side of the van. Randy blasted the horn. An answering blast followed almost immediately from deep in the lot. Over the next sixty seconds or so, blasts erupted from all the vehicles around us. But no one honked more than once, and when I'd come back to myself enough to glance at Randy, I found him counting silently.

Eight. Nine.

Before the tenth horn blast had died to echo, he punched the gear shift into drive and moved us out of the lot. My eyes flicked to the side mirror, where I saw the clown shuddering as the wind rushed over it, and beyond that, the rest of the vans falling into line in rhythmic succession.

"You always leave all together?"

Randy shrugged. "Tradition. Team-building, you know?"

"Then shouldn't I have met the rest of the team?"

"They won't be selling your ice cream."

We were headed, I realized, for the port, and for the first time, the absurd hour made a sort of sense. The workers down here had been on all night, probably shifting huge crates inside cargo containers that trapped heat like ovens.

"So what are yours?" Randy said as we crossed the Pacific Coast Highway, angling between grunting eighteen-wheelers as we approached the docks. Between trucks and stacked crates and gantry cranes, I caught glimpses of big ships hulking in the fog, their steel siding so much more solid, somehow, than the glass-and-concrete structures perched on the land behind us.

"I'm sorry?"

"You said you guessed we have different priorities. I'm not sure I liked that. I want to know what yours are."

Startled, I turned toward his enormous frame—a superfreighter to my weekend eight-footer—and decided on caution.

"Just...spread a little happiness," I said. "Get some myself. Make buttloads of money so I don't have to eat Top Ramen and bologna at the end of next semester. Maybe get laid for the first time since high school."

"See?" He sounded almost defensive as he let the van glide to a stop in front of two forklifts and some more heavy machinery I had no name for. "Happiness and money. Don't know about you, but I'm thinking I haven't had my share of either, yet."

Reaching under his seat with both hands, he pulled up the first assault rifle I had ever sat beside. It was flat black and spindly except for the chamber, or whatever it was called, that ballooned off the back of the trigger area. The barrel pointed straight at me. Randy did something that made the whole thing click, swung the stock to his shoulder and sighted down into the dash, then returned the rifle to its hiding place.

"Is that an Uzi?" I whispered.

"Not a Corps man, huh, Big Screen?"

"You were?"

"Six severely fucked-up years. Wait here. I'll introduce you properly from your own van tomorrow."

He opened his door and hopped down, assuming point position in the phalanx of van drivers that immediately formed around him. My eyes kept wandering from the phalanx to the shadows under Randy's seat to the Safety Clown crouching in the corner of the side mirror, right above the *Objects May Be Closer Than They Appear* warning. My father's ghost kept floating up in front of me, too, so it didn't occur to me that we hadn't reopened the back of the van or dug into any freezer bins until Randy returned, dropping a small, square cardboard box onto my lap.

"Count those, okay?" This time, he didn't even wait for his colleagues to reach their vehicles, and he didn't wave as we u-turned and blew by them. Seconds later, we were speeding north on the freeway.

I pried the duct tape off the top of the box. "Seemed like you trusted Jaybo," I said.

"These guys aren't Jaybo."

The box lid fell open, and I lifted out the topmost plastic baggie, zipped tight, packed with white powder that shifted when I pressed like confectioner's sugar. I knew what it was, though I'd never done any. Dazed, I started counting bags, got most of the way through, and looked up.

"How many?" Randy said. I could feel his eyes on me in the mirror.

Don't react, I thought. Don't react, don't react, *"This is fucking cocaine!"*

Randy grinned. "Appreciate the appraisal. But I need a count, there, Bubba."

My brain scrambled back to the pier. I'd barely paid atten-tion. I didn't even remember seeing anybody but Safety Clown drivers.

"Thirty-seven," I said dully.

"You're sure?"

"Thirty-eight."

"Positive?"

I nodded.

"Guess you're not going to find out what kind of rifle this is yet." The note of open disappointment in his voice drew my gaze, and my gaze made him laugh. "Got ya."

The next three hours passed in a blur. The marine layer had burned away, leaving a bottomless blue emptiness overhead. We stopped at two law offices and one dental practice in Sorrento Valley. By the time we reached the dentist's, I'd started getting nauseous and rolled my window down, which is how I got to hear the receptionist with the white, winking hair yell, "Hey, Doc. Here comes the cavalry" through the open office door.

Our next stop was Ripped Racquet and Health Gym, where a pony-tailed tai chi instructor halted the class he was conducting on the circle of grass fronting the building to stop Randy. "Hey, guy, do the clown."

"You're doing him just fine," Randy answered, then gave the instructor what looked like a brotherly chuck on the shoulder of his robe as he breezed past. He was inside almost half an hour, and when he returned, he waved at me to pass him the cardboard box from the floor. He fished out three more baggies, tucking them carefully into the waistband of his jeans. "Walk-up biz," he said happily, and trotted back indoors.

From there, we cut over to the 101 and up the coast, stopping at Del Mar Plaza and the Quesadilla Shack five minutes from my condo door, where I laid myself flat on the front seat and told Randy I was known in this place. The real reason for my hiding had more to do with the number of dinners I'd eaten with my mom on the red picnic tables in the sand outside the Shack, versus the purpose of my current visit.

Randy gave me a long look, and the fear I should have been feeling all along finally prickled down my scalp. But all he did was pat my head. "You should eat, Big Screen. I get so caught up doing this, I forget half the time. Doesn't mean you should. Want a carne asada?"

Just the thought made me gag. He came back ten minutes later with a Coke for me and nothing at all for himself.

"Okay," he said. "Ready for the good stuff?"

I leaned my head against the window and kept my eyes closed, and we drove a long time. When I finally opened my eyes again, we were juddering over a dirt road just a bit narrower than the van, crushing birds-of-paradise stalks on either side as we rumbled forward. Still nauseous, increasingly nervous, I scanned the fields and saw red and orange and blue flowers nodding like peasants at a passing lord, but no buildings anywhere. I thought of the poppy fields of Oz, the witch's voice and her green hand caressing her crystal ball. Randy downshifted, and I sat up straight as the van coasted to a stop.

No one on this planet knew where I'd gone today. Certainly, no one other than the Safety Clown people had seen me arrive downtown. *Training*, Jaybo had called it. What if it was more of a test? And I had not accompanied Randy on a single sale.

"Get out," he said quietly, and popped the locks on both our doors.

I did, considering bolting straight into the flowers. But I had little chance of outdistancing my companion. I watched him remove his not-Uzi from under his seat and step down and swing his door shut.

"Listen," I said. He was already halfway around the front of the van, using his gun machete-style to chop flowers out of his path. I'd meant to start pleading, but wound up standing still instead, gobbling up each tick of insect wing, every whisper of wind in the petals. I swear I could hear the sunlight falling.

Arriving beside me, Randy stared into the distance, dangling the rifle by the trigger-guard. For a few seconds, we stood. Above us, the blue yawned wider.

"So what do you think, Big Screen?" he said. "Just you and me?" In one motion, he swept the rifle butt to his shoulder and fired five quick bursts into the sky, which swallowed them. Then he grinned. "Better get that door open."

Before I'd even unlocked my knees and gulped new air into my lungs, people sprang from the flowers like rousted pheasants in a whirl of dark skin and tattered straw hats and threadbare work shirts open to the waist. Several of them chirped enthusiastic greetings at Randy in Spanish as I stumbled back against the van. He chirped right back.

"Hurry up, Big Screen," he barked, and I reached a trembling hand between clown slats and grabbed the handle and twisted. I was grateful I hadn't drunk any of the Coke from the Quesadilla Shack. If I'd had any liquid in me, I would just have pissed it all over my legs.

As soon as the door was open, Randy jumped in and threw back the nearest freezer lid. The field hands nuzzled closer to us like pups vying for suckling spots, though they avoided so much as nudging me. One, a boy of maybe twelve, met my eyes for a moment and murmured, "*Buenos dias.*" Several others nodded as they edged past. I climbed up next to Randy.

"*De nada*, Hector," he was saying, handing a chocolate nut Drumstick to the nearest worker, whose spiky streak of dirt-gray goatee looked embedded in his skin like a vein of ore in rock. Hector handed Randy a dime and retreated to the back of the group, peeling eagerly at the paper wrapping.

Distribution to the whole group took less than five minutes, but Randy lingered another twenty, dangling his legs out the cabin door, talking only occasionally, smiling a lot. The workers clumped in groups of two or three, leaning on hoes and wolfing down Igloo Pies while gazing over the fields. Their dwellings, I realized, might well be hidden out here somewhere, along with any other family members who'd somehow made it this far and managed to find them. None of them spoke to me again, but every single one tipped his sombrero to Randy before melting away into the fields they tended. They left neither trash nor trace.

"This stuff sold for a dollar when I was ten," I said. "And that was ten years ago." My voice sounded strained, shaky. Randy's rifle lay seemingly forgotten between freezer bins in the van behind us. I almost made a lunge for it. But I couldn't for the life of me figure what I'd do afterward.

"Cost me a buck-twenty per," Randy said. "But see, I figure I can afford it. Starting tomorrow, you can make your own decisions. Beauty of being a Safety Clown, dude. Ain't no one going to know or care but you."

Clambering inside, he collected his rifle, hunched to avoid banging his head, and began swatting freezer lids shut. He didn't seem thoughtful enough to be deciding whether to mow me down.

"Why not just give it to them?" I asked. "The ice cream, I mean."

Randy cocked his head. The gun remained tucked under one arm against his chest. "You like insulting people, Big Screen?"

I gaped at him.

"Didn't think so. Remember, they don't know what it costs me." He left me to slide the door shut again, and we rumbled out of the fields and returned to the coast.

Another two hours passed. We stopped at an antique shop and some accounting firms, a bowling alley and a retirement home. At the latter, I finally emerged from the van. Partially, I did so because I thought I'd better. Partially, I wanted to get away from the freon I'd been breathing virtually nonstop for the past eight hours, and which by now had given me a sledgehammer headache. But also, I'd gotten curious. The experience in the flower fields had shaken something loose in me, and I could feel it rattling around as I stepped into the midday heat.

Randy had already been inside fifteen minutes. I wondered if he'd received the same joyful, personal greeting there that he had everywhere else we'd gone. Edging forward, I reached the sidewalk fronting the main entrance, where my progress was blocked by a bald, pink-skinned marvel of a man whose curvature of the spine kept his head roughly level with my navel. Jabbing the legs of his metal walker into the ground like climbing pitons, the man dragged himself toward the brightly lettered sign at the edge of the parking lot that read BEACH ACCESS. Below the words on the sign was the silhouette of a longhaired bathing beauty laid out flat with her breasts poking straight up in the air. The man didn't acknowledge me as he inched past, but he did remove the cherry lollipop from his mouth, and left it hovering in front of his lips like the dot at the bottom of a kicked-over question mark. I thought about lifting him, ferrying him gently to the sand.

Only then did it occur to me that the man might well have hauled himself out here for Randy. *Help people*, my mother had commanded, since the day I first started working. But help them what? Which jobs, exactly, qualified, and who got to say?

By the time Randy returned, I'd stumbled back to my seat,

more confused than scared for the moment, and the question-mark man was well on his way to the bathing beauties.

"Two-thirty yet?" Randy asked, though he was the one with the watch. He checked it. "Right on."

Leaving the coast, he drove us across the freeway, over El Camino Real and into the maze of white and salmon-pink condo communities and housing developments that had all but enclosed the eastern rim of North and San Diego Counties during the course of my lifetime. Any one of them could have been mine. Blood beat against my temples and massed behind my forehead. I closed my eyes, caught an imaginary glimpse of my mother bent over her potted plants at the nursery where she'd worked, better paid and sunscreened than the workers in the flower fields but nearly as invisible, and opened my eyes again to find Randy's hand hurtling toward my chest.

I twisted aside, but he didn't seem to notice, just grabbed the knob on the dash that I'd assumed was a glove box handle. Now I realized there was no glove box. Randy twisted the knob to the right.

At first, nothing happened. Then the air shattered into winking, tinkling shards of sound. My hands rose uselessly to my ears, then dropped again. The van slowed, stopped on the curve of a cul-de-sac, and Randy shouldered his door open, nearly banging his head on the ceiling as he jumped out and rubbed his hands together.

"Watch the master, Big Screen. Learn." Striding around front, he stood with his hands on his hips, gazing into the yards like a gunslinger as the sound rained down on him. Then he bounded around the van, pulled open my door, flicked the lever on the control panel, and danced backward as the clown leapt off its stilts and started unfolding.

I staggered from the van as the first children of the entire day swept around the curve of the cul-de-sac on their skateboards and bore down on us. My ears finally filtered enough distortion for me to register the tune the van was blaring.

"*Classical Gas?*" I babbled, as Randy stepped carefully

around the clown. It hung still now, STOP sign jabbed over the street.

"What about it?" Randy threw open the sliding door and began pulling up multiple bin lids.

To my amazement, I felt my lips slip upwards. "I've got a friend who claims this is the only music on earth it's impossible to make a girl have an orgasm to."

If my own smile surprised me, Randy's nearly blew me backward with its brightness. "Wish I had enough experience or knowledge to challenge that statement. Always been kind of shy, myself. And lately, I've been too busy making money. My *man*, Joel."

He stuck one huge hand past me, and the first skateboard kid to reach the van smacked it with his own. "Pop Rocket, Randy," the kid said, straightening the cargo shorts from which his watermelon-striped boxers billowed.

"Cherry, right?" Randy had already handed the kid his popsicle without waiting for an answer. "What-up, Empire?"

The reasons for that nickname never revealed themselves to me. What became immediately apparent, though, was how much this second kid liked that Randy knew it. He gave his board a kick-hop and wrapped it in his arms and stood close to the van, looking proud, as Randy gave him his ice cream. By the time that group had departed, twelve more kids, ranging in age from maybe five to no younger than me, had emerged from houses or backyards or neighboring streets. No one seemed to mind the racket roaring out of the rooftop speaker, and a few customers even turned their bodies and faces to it, arms outstretched, eyes closed, as though accepting a cooling blast from a garden hose. Every single person knew Randy's name, and he knew most of theirs.

"You Randy's new helper?" said a soft voice so close to my ear that I thought for a second it had come from inside me.

Turning, I found myself confronting a freckle-faced girl of maybe fifteen, with a yellow drugstore Wiffle bat over her bare shoulder. Self-consciously, she wound the wild strands of her strawberry-blonde hair back into her scrunchy with sweaty fingers. Her eyes, green and soft as the squares of over-watered lawn fronting the houses of this block, never left mine.

Too much time passed, and I had no answer. I wanted to borrow her bat, dare her to try to pitch a ball past me. I also wanted her to stop flirting with me because she was too young and only adding to my anxiety. I thought of my mom peering down from the Heaven she didn't believe in, and had to smother competing impulses to wave and whimper.

"You should be," the girl finally said, in that same breathy voice. "Hey, Randy." From her pocket, she withdrew a wad of bills, palmed them, and passed them into the van. Randy ducked inside and returned with a baggie, which disappeared into the girl's shorts pocket.

"Go easy, Carolina," said Randy. "Say hi to your sis."

The girl wandered away, wiggling her bat once at both or neither of us.

I sat down on the curb under the Safety Clown's arm, and the sunlight dropped on my shoulders like a sandbag. For the first time, I let myself ask the question. *Could I do this? Did I want to*? It'd pay for next semester, all right. And it would certainly qualify as a story to tell. Once the statute of limitations ran out.

We were close to an hour in that one cul-de-sac, then nearly two in the fire lane of the circular parking lot of a little league complex with four grassless fields that looked stripped bare like shaved cats. Kids just kept coming. Mostly, they bought ice cream. Every now and then, one or a little group would lurk until a lull came, then dart or sidle or just stride forward and pop $75 or sometimes an envelope into Randy's hands.

At one point, feeling oddly jealous as yet another group of kids clustered around and jabbered at Randy, I asked him, "What happens if you're not sure?"

"What's that, Big Screen?"

"What if it's a kid you don't know? You wouldn't want to make a mistake."

"Oh." He turned to me, grinning. "I've got a system."

Not twenty minutes later, I got to see the system in action. The kid in question looked about eleven, despite the pimples peppering his forehead and leaning off the end of his nose. He hovered near the swing-set just off the parking lot, sweating and jumpy in his long-sleeved, webbed Spider-Man shirt. Finally, he came forward, eyes everywhere.

Randy glanced at me, mouthing *Watch this*. Then he stepped from the van to meet the kid, folding his arms across his cliff of a chest, and said, "Yo, friend. What's your name?"

"Zach."

"Yo, Zach. Did you need ice cream or…*ice cream?*"

I stared at Randy's back. He swung his head around and beamed proudly before returning full attention to his customer.

"Ice cream," the kid said, flung $75 into Randy's hands, and fled with his treat.

Randy employed exactly the same technique a little later with a pale, teenaged girl with black lipstick and what appeared to be at least five different henna tattoos applied one on top of another on her bare ankles under her long skirt. The resulting mess looked like hieroglyphics, or a gang tag. When Randy asked his question, her mouth unhinged, as though he'd bonked her on the head. He gave her two Drumsticks for her dollar, called it his "Welcome to Randy Special," and directed me to shut down the music and reel in the clown. I did both, leaned out the window to watch the clown fold, and nearly slammed into the scowling woman's face with my own.

She wore a navy blue button-up shirt, tight blue slacks, and for a second, I thought she was a cop. She'd pulled her red hair back so tightly that the wrinkles in her forehead seemed to be splitting open. As I stared, gargling, she banged my door with her hand, rattling the clown on its stilts. Beside me, Randy settled into the driver's seat. Then his hand crossed my chest and pushed me gently back against the peeling vinyl.

"Ma'am. Something I can get you?" Randy asked.

"How about a brain?" the woman hissed. "How about a conscience?"

"Now, ma'am, I'm sure you have both those things."

The woman nearly spat in our faces, and my legs started shaking. Abruptly, my head jerked sideways, checking for Randy's other hand. It was on the steering wheel, not feeling around under his seat. And on his face was a smile gentler than any I'd seen all day.

"That's your natural color, isn't it?" He didn't even turn the key in the ignition. "Beautiful. Almost maroon."

"Ever seen someone die, Mr. Smarty-Arty Ice Cream Man? I have. When I was nine years old. Janitor at my school. Want to know why he died? Because some service asshole like you was parked in the fire lane and the ambulance couldn't get up the driveway."

Randy made a *pop* with his cheeks. "Right," he said. "Absolutely right. I'm sorry, and it won't happen again."

The woman blinked, hand half-raised as though she might slap the van again. Instead, she shook her head and stalked off.

"Never understand it," Randy murmured, starting the van. "Why are moral people always so angry?" Pulling out of the lot, he glanced my way, saw me ramrod straight against the seatback with my legs still trembling together. "Know many people like that, Big Screen?"

My tongue felt impossibly dry, as though it had been wrung. "Um." I put my hands on my legs, held them until they quieted. "I think I thought I was one."

"You?" Randy grinned. Then without warning he reached out and patted me on the head. "Not you, Big Screen. You don't have it in you. And you don't treat people that way. Trust your buddy Big Randy."

We stayed out four more hours. Around six, Randy began cruising family pizza restaurants, the multi-plex lot just before the 7:30 shows, a 24-hour workout gym where he sold only ice cream (no *ice cream*) to exhausted soccer parents and desk-drones desperately stretching their bodies. Most of these people knew Randy's name, too.

Finally, a little after nine, on a residential street overlooking

Moonlight Beach, Randy shut off the van, then turned to me. Out on the water, even the moon seemed to be burrowing a straight, white trail to his door.

"You haven't eaten a single goddamn thing, have you, Big Screen? I'm sorry about that." Almost as an afterthought, his hands slipped under the seat between his legs and came up with the rifle.

My breath caught, but by this point I was too tired to hold it. "You either," I murmured, watching his hands.

"Yeah, but…you'll see. Tomorrow. There's this charge people give off when you're not judging them, just giving them what they want and letting them be. It's a physical thing, man. It pours out of their eyes, and it's more filling than any food. I'm so charged, most days, I barely even sleep. Not to mention richer."

It was true. I'd watched it happen all day. I wasn't sure anyone in my entire life had ever been as pleased to see me as Randy's customers were to see him. And he felt the same way.

The rifle slid into his lap, muzzle aimed just over my legs at the center of the door. "You'll be back?" His voice bore no apparent threat.

Eventually, when I'd said nothing for long enough, Randy nodded. "You'll be back. You're the thoughtful sort. Like I said."

"Does it ever bother you?" I asked.

Randy stared at me, and the moon lit him. "Does what?"

Dropping the rifle back in its place, he drove us straight to the freeway and back downtown. He didn't turn on the radio or say another word. White and red reflections from the dashboard and passing cars flared in his skin like sparks.

In the lot, we found all the other vans not just parked but empty, clowns locked into cockroach position at their sides. A single low light burned in Jaybo's trailer. I wondered if he lived there, then why he would. He had to have plenty of money.

"Go home, Big Screen," Randy told me as soon as he'd backed the van into its space at the head of the right-hand row. "I've got to wipe out the bins and finish up. You get some food and sleep."

I didn't argue. My head hurt, and a loneliness less specific—and therefore all the more suffocating—than any I'd experienced before crept into my chest and filled my lungs. And yet I found myself turning to Randy, who flashed me his blinding, affect-less smile. I thought he might burst into one last chorus. *We'll all have chicken and dumplings when she comes.* But he just smiled.

The only thing I could think to say was, "Looks like we're the last ones back."

"Always. Going to give me a run, Big Screen?"

Slipping from my seat, I stood blinking on the pavement while the fast-cooling air pushed my grinding teeth apart and drove some of the deadness out. My fingertips began tingling, then stinging, as though I'd just come in from sledding. I was trying to remember where I'd parked my car—could it really have been earlier today?—when the door of Jaybo's Airstream opened and his goldfish eyes peered toward me. I froze.

"Max?" Out he came. His shorts had flowers on them. Maybe all Safety Clown employees slept here. In their vans. In the freezer bins, which doubled as coffins.

"You have a good time, son? Learn a lot?"

"Tired," I managed, watching him, listening for any sign of Randy stepping out to trap me between them.

"Randy's a madman." Jaybo smiled. "No one expects you to work like that. But I thought you'd enjoy learning from the best. Like my clowns?"

I resisted the urge to look at one and shook my head.

Jaybo's smile got wider. "Got to admit they're memorable, though. Knew they'd be our logo, our signature, as soon as I saw them."

"Loubob's. Right?"

"You know Loubob's? See, I knew it, Max. No one comes to us by accident. I went there looking for belts and hoses for these babies." He waved his stump at the vans. "And there were the clowns just lying in a heap. I asked what they were, and he says, "'*Project. Didn't work.*' Ever heard Loubob speak?"

I shook my head again, checked Randy's van but saw no sign of him, just the passenger door hanging ajar. Jaybo took another step closer. "Not many have. I got the whole lot for 50 bucks."

To his left, at the very end of the row, one of the clowns had come open, or been left that way. In the shadows, at this distance, I couldn't see its face, but it was shivering like a scarecrow in the salty ocean breeze.

"See ya," I heard myself say.

"Tomorrow. Right?"

Without answering, I turned, waiting for the rush of footsteps or flick of a rifle safety-catch, and started for the street. Just as I reached the gate, I heard a thud from Randy's van, couldn't help turning, and found Randy's face filling the windshield. When he saw me looking, he pressed one gorilla-sized hand to the glass, fingers open. Waving. I got in my car and drove home.

I'd tiptoed halfway up the entry stairs before remembering it would take more than that to wake my mother. I made myself a tuna sandwich and ate a third of it, seeing Randy's last wave, his wide-open grin. The condo felt even emptier than it had for the past month. Even the ghost of my father's smell had drained from the walls. My mother had left no smell, ghostly or otherwise. I crawled off to bed and miraculously slept until after four before bolting awake hyperventilating.

Flipping onto my stomach, I curled into myself like a caterpillar and managed, after ten minutes of total panic, to get myself calmed enough to start to think.

As far as I could tell, I had three choices. I could get up and join Jaybo and Randy and the gang spreading joy, ice cream, and *ice cream* throughout San Diego County, have a hundred or more people of all ages and types rush out to greet me by name whenever they saw me, and make more money in a couple months than my mom had in any one decade of her life. I could call the police, pray they found and arrested all Sunshine Safety Clown employees, and then spend the rest of my days hoping none of them got out, ever. Or I could do neither, hide here in the fog with the horses and hope Jaybo understood the absence of both me and the police as the don't-ask-don't-tell bargain I was offering.

Instead of choosing, I got sick.

For the first few hours, I figured I was faking it, or manufacturing it, anyway. Then, when the chills started, I dug around in my mother's bathroom, found a thermometer in the otherwise empty cosmetic drawer, and checked myself. I got a reading of 102, climbed back into bed, and stayed there two days.

No one called. No one knocked at the door. No one parked by the complex's sauna and played a blast of *Classical Gas*. Around midnight of the second night, the phone rang, and I dragged myself out of bed. Passing my mother's doorway, I half-believed I could see her tucked into her usual corner in the king-sized bed she'd once shared with my father, not moving or breathing, as though she'd snuck out of her grave to get warm.

The fever, I realized, had gone. Beneath my feet, the hardwood floor felt cool, the air gentle against my itching legs. This was just the world, after all. Big, thoroughly mapped place to sell joy or buy it, hunt company or flee it, trust yourself or your friends or your instincts, stretch the hours as much as you could, and one day vanish.

Pulling my mother's door shut, I padded into the living room and picked up the receiver just before the sixth ring, beating the answering machine. But on the other end I found only electrical hum and a distant clacking sound.

The next morning, I got up, broke eggs into a pan, and flipped on the pocket television on the counter for company. Then I stood, staring, wet yolk dripping from the end of my wooden spoon onto my mother's once-spotless hardwood floor.

Under a flashing banner that read *LIVE—BREAKING NEWS*, a camera scanned a downtown parking lot. Red and blue lights flashed and reflected in the windows of ten white vans, illuminating what looked like spatters of mud all over their metal sides and grills.

"Once again, a scene of incredible, despicable violence downtown

this morning as police discover the apparent massacre and dismember-
ment of as many as fifteen employees of the Sunshine Safety Clown ice
cream truck company. Police have long targeted the company as the key
element in a major Southland drug trafficking ring, and department
spokesmen confirm that this vicious mass slaying appears to be drug
related. No additional specifics either about the trafficking ring or the
nature and timing of the murders have been released as yet."

I put my hand down almost inside the frying pan, jerked
back, and knocked egg everywhere. My eyes never left the
screen.

"We've had our eyes on these people for months," a police
department spokesman was saying, as the camera prowled
jerkily, restlessly behind him, capturing lights, an open van door,
a helicopter overhead, body bags. More lights. "Arrests were
forthcoming. Imminent, in fact. We're disappointed and also,
obviously, horrified. An attack of this ferocity is unprecedented in this
county. These people are savages, and they must be rooted out of our
city."

"Randy," I whispered, surprised that I did.

Suddenly, I was bent forward, so close to the tiny screen that
it seemed I could climb into it. I waited until the camera pulled
back to scan the lot again.

Then I was out the door, not even buckling my sandals until
I'd driven the Geo screeching out of the condo lot to the bottom
of the hill to wait for the endless, stupid light at the lip of the
freeway onramp. Traffic clogged the interstate, and I was nearly
an hour getting downtown, but I don't remember thinking a
single thing during all that time except that I had to have seen it
wrong. The cameras just hadn't showed everything. Even the
idea was juvenile, an idiotic thing to be thinking about right this
moment.

What I should have done was go to the police. Instead, I
parked as close as I could to the temporary barriers the cops had
erected, edged through the block-long crowd of gawkers, got the
single glimpse I needed to confirm what the cameras had
already shown me, then very nearly shoved people to the

ground as I forced my way back out. My breath was a barbed thing, catching in the lining of my throat and tearing it. An older Hispanic woman in a yellow shawl threw her arm around me and made comforting *shush*-ing sounds. I shook her off.

What I'd seen was blood, all right, splashed all over the vans, coating the wheel wells and even some of the windows. I'd seen doors flung open, some wrenched half off their hinges. What I hadn't seen were clowns. Not a single one, anywhere. Just the wooden frames where they'd hung like bats to sleep off the daylight.

I drove around and around downtown in a sort of crazy circle, Hillcrest, India Street, Laurel, Broadway, South Street, the harbor, the Gaslamp, back again. The clowns had been taken off, obviously. Ripped free in the fray, or pried away by police for easier van access. This was just another deflection, like my two-day fever, from having to deal with my own culpability. Then I thought of muffler men peering around trees. And I remembered the midnight phone call I'd received last night. Sometime in the late afternoon, I stopped the car, wobbled into a pay phone booth, dialed information, paid the extra fifty cents and let the computer connect me.

The phone in Loubobland's junkyard rang and rang. I let it, leaning my forehead against the sun-warmed glass, sensing the ocean scant blocks away, beating quietly underneath the boats and pilings.

Several seconds passed before I realized my call had been answered, that I was listening to silence. No one had spoken, but someone was there.

"The clowns," I croaked.

The person on the other end grunted. "I have nothing to say."

"Just one question." I was blurting the words, trying to fit them in before he hung up. "The project."

"What?"

"You told Jaybo the clowns were a failed project. I just want to know what it was."

Silence. But no dial tone. I heard fumbling, for a match, maybe. Then a long, hitching breath. "Neighborhood watch," Loubob said, and hung up.

That was five hours ago. Since then, I've been holed up in my mother's condo—it will never, could never be mine—thinking mostly about Randy. About his *Coming 'Round the Mountain* whistle and his electric shock of joy-giving, his hand against the windshield as he waved goodbye. I hadn't been considering joining them, I thought. Not really. Not quite.

But I hadn't called the cops, either. Because I was scared, maybe. But mostly because I hadn't wanted to, wasn't so sure who was doing good, being useful, making lives easier. And I'd liked the way they treated each other, the Safety Clown family. And Randy…I think Randy took me for his friend. Maybe I could have been.

So I'd let them be. And the clowns had come.

I've got the blinds thrown wide, but I can't see a blessed thing out there through the fog and dark. I've kept the TV off, listening instead to the air-conditioning, while I wonder for the thousandth time if I was supposed to have called the police, and whether that would have saved anyone. Or me.

Tomorrow, maybe the next day, if no one comes, I'm going to have to get up. Maybe I'll go to the cops, and let them laugh. I've got to find another job if I'm going to go to school, have a life. But for now, I'm staying right here, in what's left of the place I grew up in, holding my knees, while my ears strain for the clacking I heard on the phone two nights ago, the clatter of footless wooden legs on stairs that will tell me once and for all if what I do matters, and whether there's really such thing as a line, and whether I crossed it.

Devil's Smile

"In hollows of the liquid hills
Where the long Blue Ridges run
The flatter of no echo thrills
For echo the seas have none;
Nor aught that gives man back man's strain—
The hope of his heart, the dream in his brain."
— Herman Melville

Turning in his saddle, Selkirk peered behind him through the flurrying snow, trying to determine which piece of debris had lamed his horse. All along what had been the carriage road, bits of driftwood, splintered sections of hull and harpoon handle, discarded household goods—pans, candlesticks, broken-backed books, empty lanterns—and at least one section of long, bleached-white jaw lay half-buried in the sand. The jaw still had baleen attached, and bits of blown snow had stuck in it, which made it look more recently alive than it should have.

Selkirk rubbed his tired eyes against the gray December morning and hunched deeper into his inadequate long coat as the wind whistled off the whitecaps and sliced between the dunes. The straw hat he wore—more out of habit than hope of protection—did nothing to warm him, and stray blond curls kept whipping across his eyes. Easing himself from the horse, Selkirk dropped to the sand.

He should have conducted his business here months ago. His surveying route for the still-fledgling United States Lighthouse Service had taken him in a crisscrossing loop from the tip of the Cape all the way up into Maine and back.

He'd passed within fifty miles of Cape Roby Light and its singular keeper twice this fall, and both times had continued on. Why? Because Amalia had told him the keeper's tale on the night he'd imagined she loved him? Or maybe he just hated coming back here even more than he thought he would. For all he knew, the keeper had long since moved on, dragging her memories behind her. She might even have died. So many had, around here. Setting his teeth against the wind, Selkirk wrapped his frozen fingers in his horse's bridle and led her the last down-sloping mile and a half into Winsett.

Entering from the east, he saw a scatter of stone and clapboard homes and boarding houses hunched against the dunes, their windows dark. None of them looked familiar. Like so many of the little whaling communities he'd visited during his survey, the town he'd known had simply drained away into the burgeoning, bloody industry centers at New Bedford and Nantucket.

Selkirk had spent one miserable fall and winter here fourteen years ago, sent by his drunken father to learn candle-making from his drunken uncle. He'd accepted the nightly open-fisted beatings without comment, skulking afterward down to the Blubber Pike tavern to watch the whalers: the Portuguese swearing loudly at each other, and the negroes—so many negroes, most of them recently freed, more than a few newly escaped—clinging in clumps to the shadowy back tables and stealing fearful glances at every passing face, as though they expected at any moment to be spirited away.

Of course, there'd been his cousin, Amalia, for all the good that had ever done him. She'd just turned eighteen at the time, two years his senior. Despite her blonde hair and startling fullness, the Winsett whalers had already learned to steer clear, but for some reason, she'd liked Selkirk. At least, she'd liked needling him about his outsized ears, his floppy hair, the crack in his voice he could not outgrow. Whatever the reason, she'd lured him away from the pub on several occasions to stare at the moon and drink beside him. Once, in a driving sleet, she'd led him on a midnight walk to Cape Roby Point. There, lurking uncomfortably close but never touching him, standing on the rocks with her dark eyes cocked like rifle sights at the rain, she'd told him the lighthouse keeper's story. At the end, without any explanation, she'd turned, opened her heavy coat and pulled him to her. He'd had no idea what she wanted him to do, and had wound up simply setting his ear against her slicked skin, all but tasting the water that rushed into the valley between her breasts, listening to her heart banging way down inside her.

After that, she'd stopped speaking to him entirely. He'd knocked on her door, chased her half out of the shop one morning and been stopped by a chop to the throat from his uncle, left notes peeking out from under the rug outside her room. She'd responded to none of it, and hadn't even bothered to say goodbye when he left. Selkirk had steered clear of all women for more than a decade afterward, except for the very occasional company he paid for near the docks where he slung cargo, until the Lighthouse Service offered him an unexpected escape.

Now, half-dragging his horse down the empty main street, Selkirk found he couldn't even remember which grim room the Blubber Pike had been. He passed no one. But at the western edge of the frozen, cracking main thoroughfare, less than a block from where his uncle had kept his establishment, he found a traveler's stable and entered.

The barn was lit by banks of horseshoe-shaped wall sconces—apparently, local whale oil or no, candles remained in ready supply—and a coal fire glowed in the open iron stove at the rear of the barn. A dark-haired stable lad with a clam-shaped birthmark covering his left cheek and part of his forehead appeared from one of the stables in the back, *tsked* over Selkirk's injured mount, and said he'd send for the horse doctor as soon as he'd got the animal dried and warmed and fed.

"Still a horse doctor here?" Selkirk asked.

The boy nodded.

Selkirk paid the boy and thanked him, then wandered toward the stove and stood with his hands extended to the heat, which turned them purplish red. If he got about doing what should have been done years ago, he'd be gone by nightfall, providing his horse could take him. From his memory of the midnight walk with Amalia, Cape Roby Point couldn't be more than three miles away. Once at the lighthouse, if its longtime occupant did indeed still live there, he'd brook no romantic nonsense—neither his own, nor the keeper's. The property did not belong to her, was barely suitable for habitation, and its lack both of updated equipment and experienced, capable attendant posed an undue and unacceptable threat to any ship unlucky enough to hazard past. Not that many bothered anymore with this particular stretch of abandoned, storm-battered coast.

Out he went into the snow. In a matter of minutes, he'd left Winsett behind. Head down, he burrowed through the gusts. With neither buildings nor dunes to block it, the wind raked him with bits of shell and sand that clung to his cheeks like the tips of fingernails and then ripped free. When he looked up, he saw beach pocked with snow and snarls of seaweed, then the ocean thrashing about between the shore and the sandbar a hundred yards or so out.

An hour passed. More. The tamped-down path, barely discernible during Winsett's heyday, had sunk completely into the shifting earth. Selkirk stepped through stands of beach heather and sand bur, pricking himself repeatedly about the ankles. Eventually, he felt blood beneath one heavy sock, but he didn't peel the sock back, simply yanked out the most accessible spines and kept moving. Far out to sea, bright, yellow sun flickered in the depths of the cloud cover and vanished as suddenly as it had appeared. *Devil's smile,* as the Portuguese sailors called that particular effect. At the time, it hadn't occurred to Selkirk to ask why the light would be the devil, instead of the dark or the gathering storm. Stepping from the V between two leaning dunes, he saw the lighthouse.

He'd read the report from the initial Lighthouse Service survey three years ago, and more than once. That document mentioned rot in every beam, chips and cracks in the bricks that made up the conical tower, erosion all around the foundation. As far as Selkirk could see, the report had been kind. The building seemed to be crumbling to nothing before his eyes, bleeding into the pool of shorewater churning at the rocks beneath it.

Staring into the black tide racing up the sand to meet him, Selkirk caught a sea tang on his tongue and found himself murmuring a prayer he hadn't planned for Amalia, who'd reportedly wandered into the dunes and vanished one winter night, six years after Selkirk left. Her father had written Selkirk's father that the girl had never had friends, hated him, hated Winsett, and was probably happier wherever she was now. Then he'd said, *'Here's what I hope: that she's alive. And that she's somewhere far from anywhere I will ever be.'*

On another night than the one they'd spent out here, somewhere closer to town but similarly deserted, he and Amalia once found themselves beset by gulls that swept out of the moonlight all together, by the hundreds, as though storming the mainland. Amalia had pitched stones at them, laughing as they shrieked and swirled nearer. Finally, she'd hit one in the head and killed it. Then she'd bent over the body, calling Selkirk to her. He'd expected her to cradle it or cry. Instead, she'd dipped her finger in its blood and painted a streak down Selkirk's face. Not her own.

Looking down now, Selkirk watched the tide reach the tips of his boots again. How much time had he wasted during his dock-working years imagining—hoping—that Amalia might be hidden behind some stack of crates or in a nearby alley, having sought him out after leaving Winsett?

Angry now, Selkirk picked his way between rocks to the foot of the tower. A surge of whitewater caught him off guard and pasted his trousers to his legs, and the wind promptly froze them with a gust.

Up close, the tower looked even worse. Most of the bricks had crumbled and whitened, the salt air creating blotchy lesions like leper spots all over them. The main building still stood straight enough, but even from below, with the wind whipping the murky winter light around, Selkirk could see filth filming the windows that surrounded the lantern room, and cracks in the glass.

The keeper's quarters squatted to the left of the light tower, and looked, if possible, even more disheveled. Along the base, lime had taken hold, sprouting up the wooden walls. This would not be somewhere the Service salvaged. Cape Roby Light would have to come down, or simply be abandoned to the sea.

Selkirk rapped hard on the heavy oak door of the tower. For answer, he got a blast of wind nearly powerful enough to tip him off the rocks. Grunting, he rapped harder. Behind him, the water gurgled, the way spermaceti oil sometimes did as it bubbled, and though he knew it wasn't possible, Selkirk would have sworn he could smell it, that faint but nauseating reek his uncle assured him was imaginary. That was the glory of spermaceti oil, after all, the whole goddamn point: it had no significant odor. Every day of that dismal fall, though, Selkirk's nostrils had filled anyway. Blood, whale brain, desiccated fish. He began to pound.

Just before the door opened, he became aware of movement behind it, the slap of shoed feet descending stone steps. But he didn't stop knocking until the oak swung away from him, the light rushing not out from the lighthouse but in from the air.

He knew right away this was her, though he'd never actually seen her. Her black hair twisted over her shoulders and down her back in tangled strands like vines, just as Amalia had described. He'd expected a wild, white-haired, wind-ravaged thing, bent with age and the grief she could not shake. But of course, if Amalia's story had been accurate, this woman had been all of twenty during Selkirk's year here, and so barely over eighteen when she'd been widowed. She gazed at him now through royal blue eyes that seemed set into the darkness behind her like the last sunlit patches in a blackening sky.

"Mrs. Marchant," he said. "I'm Robert Selkirk from the Lighthouse Service. May I come in?"

For a moment, he thought she might shut the door in his face. Instead, she hovered, both arms lifting slightly from her sides. Her skirt was long, her blouse pale yellow, clinging to her square and powerful shoulders.

"Selkirk," she said. "From Winsett?"

Astonished, Selkirk started to raise his hand. Then he shook his head. "From the Lighthouse Service. But yes, I was nephew to the Winsett Selkirks."

"Well," she said, the Portuguese tilt to her words stirring memories of the Blubber Pike whalers, the smoke and the smell in there. Abruptly, she grinned. "Then you're welcome here."

"You may not feel that way in a few minutes, Mrs. Marchant. I'm afraid I've come to…"

But she'd stepped away from the door and started back up the stairs, beckoning him without turning around. Over her shoulder, he heard her say, "You must be frozen. I have tea."

In he went, and stood still in the entryway, listening to the whistling in the walls, feeling drafts rushing at him from all directions. If it weren't for the roof, the place would hardly qualify as a dwelling anymore, let alone a lifesaving beacon and refuge. He started after the woman up the twisting stairs.

Inside, too, the walls had begun to flake and mold, and the air flapped overhead as though the whole place were full of nesting birds. Four steps from the platform that filled the lantern room, just at the edge of the spill of yellow candlelight from up there, Selkirk slowed, then stopped. His gaze swung to his right and down toward his feet.

Sitting against the wall, with her little porcelain feet sticking out of the bottom of her habit and crossed at the ankle, sat a nun. From beneath the hood of the doll's black veil, disconcertingly blue eyes peered from under long lashes. A silver crucifix lay in the doll's lap, and miniature rosary beads trailed back down the steps, winking pale yellow and pink in the flickering light like seashells underwater. In fact, Selkirk realized, they *were* bits of shell.

Glancing behind him, Selkirk spotted the other dolls he'd somehow missed. All nuns. One for every other stair, on alternating walls. The others were made mostly from shell, as far as he could tell. Two of them were standing, while a third sat with her legs folded underneath her and a stone tucked against her ear, as though she were listening. At the top of the steps, still another nun dangled from her curved, seashell hands on the decaying wooden banister. Not only were her eyes blue, but also she was grinning like a little girl. Momentarily baffled to silence, Selkirk stumbled the rest of the way up to the lantern room. There, he froze completely.

Even on this dark day, even through the dust and salt that caked the window glass inside and out, light pierced the chamber. None of it came from the big lamp, which of course lay unlit. Assuming it still worked at all. Across the platform, a pair of white wicker chairs sat side by side, aimed out to sea. Over their backs, the keeper had draped blankets of bright red wool, and beneath them lay a rug of similar red. On the rug stood a house.

Like most of the dolls, it had been assembled entirely from shells and seaweed and sand. From its peaked roof, tassels of purple flowers hung like feathers, and around the eves, gull feathers hung like the decorative flourishes on some outrageous society woman's hat. On the rug—clearly, it served as a yard—tiny nuns prowled like cats. Some lay on their backs with their arms folded across their crucifixes, soaking up the light. One was climbing the leg of one of the wicker chairs. And a group—at least five—stood at the base of the window, staring out to sea.

And that is what reminded Selkirk of his purpose, and brought him at least part way back to himself. He glanced around the rest of the room, noting half a dozen round wooden tables evenly spaced around the perimeter. On each, yellow beeswax candles blazed in their candlesticks, lending the air a misleading tint of yellow and promising more heat than actually existed. Mostly, the tables held doll-making things: tiny silver crosses, multi-colored rocks, thousands of shells. The table directly to Selkirk's right had a single place-setting laid out neatly upon it: clean white plate, fork, spoon, one chipped teacup decorated with paintings of leaping silver fish.

Selkirk realized he was staring at a crude sort of living sundial. Each day, Mrs. Marchant began with her tea and breakfast, proceeded around the platform to assemble and place her nuns, spent far too long sitting in one or the other of the wicker chairs and staring at the place where it had all happened. In spite of himself, he felt a surprisingly strong twinge of pity.

"That hat can't have helped you much," Mrs. Marchant said, straightening from a bureau near her dining table where she apparently kept her tea things. The cup she brought matched the one on her breakfast table, flying fish, chips and all, and chattered lightly on its saucer as she handed it to him.

More grateful for its warmth than he realized, Selkirk rushed the cup to his mouth and winced as the hot liquid scalded his tongue. The woman stood a little too close to him. Loose strands of her hair almost tickled the back of his hand like the fringe on a shawl. Her blue eyes flicked over his face. Then she started laughing.

"What?" Selkirk took an uncertain half-step back.

"The fish," she said. When he stared, she laughed again and gestured at the cup. "When you drank, it looked like they were going to leap right into your teeth."

Selkirk glanced at the side of the cup, then back to the woman's laughing face. Judging by the layout and contents of this room, he couldn't imagine her venturing anywhere near town, but she clearly got outside to collect supplies. As a result, her skin had retained its dusky continental coloration. A beautiful creature, and no mistake.

"I am sorry," she said, meeting his eyes. "It's been a long time since anyone drank from my china but me. An unfamiliar sight. Come." She started around the left side of the platform. Selkirk watched, then took the opposite route, past the seaweed table, and met the woman at the wicker chairs on the seaward side of the platform. Without waiting for him, she bent, lifted a tiny nun whose bandeau hid most of her face off the rug, and settled in the right-hand chair. The doll wound up tucked against her hip like a pet rabbit.

For whom, Selkirk wondered, was the left-hand chair meant, on ordinary days? The obvious answer chilled and also saddened him, and he saw no point in wasting further time.

"Mrs. Marchant—"

"Manners, Mr. Selkirk," the woman said, and for the second time smiled at him. "The Sisters do not approve of being lectured to."

It took him a moment to understand she was teasing him. And not like Amalia had, or not exactly like. He sat.

"Mrs. Marchant, I have bad news. Actually, it isn't really bad news, but it may feel that way at first. I know—that is, I really think I have a sense—of what this place must mean to you. I did live in Winsett once, and I do know your story. But it's not good for you, staying here. And there are more important considerations than you or your grief here, anyway, aren't there? There are the sailors still out there braving the seas, and..."

Mrs. Marchant cocked her head, and her eyes trailed over his face so slowly that he almost thought he could feel them, faintly, like the moisture in the air but warmer.

"Would you remove your hat, Mr. Selkirk?"

Was she teasing now? She wasn't smiling. Increasingly flustered, Selkirk settled the teacup on the floor at his feet and pulled his sopping hat from his head. Instantly, his poodle's ruff of curls spilled onto his forehead and over his ears.

Mrs. Marchant sat very still. "I'd forgotten," she finally said. "Isn't that funny?"

"Ma'am?"

Sighing, she leaned back. "Men's hair by daylight." Then she winked at him, and whispered, "The Sisters are scandalized."

"Mrs. Marchant. The time has come. The Lighthouse Service—perhaps you've heard of it—needs to—"

"We had a dog, then," Mrs. Marchant said, and her eyes swung toward the windows.

Selkirk closed his eyes, feeling the warmth of the tea unfurling in his guts. When he opened his eyes again, he found Mrs. Marchant still staring toward the horizon.

"We named the dog Luis. For my father, who died at sea while my mother and I were on our way here from Lisbon. Charlie gave him to me."

After that, Selkirk hardly moved. It wasn't the story, which Amalia had told him, and which he hadn't forgotten. It was the way this woman said her husband's name.

"He didn't have to work, you know. Charlie. His family built half the boats that ever left this place. He said he just wanted to make certain his friends got home. Also, I think he liked living in the lighthouse. Especially alone with me. And my girls. The nuns, I mean."

"Smart fellow," Selkirk murmured, realized to his amazement that he'd said it aloud, and blushed.

But the keeper simply nodded. "Yes. He was. Also reckless, in a way. No, that's wrong. He liked...playing at recklessness. In storms, he used to lash himself to the railing out there." She gestured toward the thin band of metal that encircled the platform outside the windows. "Then he would lean into the rain. He said it was like sailing without having to hunt. And without leaving me."

"Was he religious like you?"

Mrs. Marchant looked completely baffled.

"The..." Selkirk muttered, and gestured at the rug, the dolls, the little shell-house. Sand-convent. Whatever it was.

"Oh," she said. "That is a habit, only." Again, she grinned, but unlike Amalia, she waited until she was certain he'd gotten the joke. Then she went on. "While my father was here, my mother and I earned extra money at home making dolls for the Sacred Heart of Mary. They gave them to poor children. Poorer than we were."

The glow from Mrs. Marchant's eyes intensified on his cheek, as though he'd leaned nearer to a candle flame. Somehow the feeling annoyed him, made him nervous.

"But he did leave you," he said, more harshly than he intended. "Your husband."

Mrs. Marchant's lips flattened slowly. "He meant to take me.

The Kendall brothers—Kit was his best and oldest friend, and he'd known Kevin since the day Kevin was born—wanted us both to come sail with them, on the only beautiful January weekend I have ever experienced here. 1837. The air was so warm, Mr. Selkirk, and the whales gone for the winter. I didn't realize until then that Charlie had never once, in his whole life, been to sea. I'd never known until that weekend that he wanted to go. Of course I said yes. Then Luis twisted his foreleg in the rocks out there, and I stayed to be with him. And I made Charlie go anyway. He was blond like you. Did you know that?"

Shifting in his seat, Selkirk stared over the water. The sky hung heavy and low, its color an unbroken blackish gray, so that he no longer had any idea what time it was. After noon, surely. If he failed to conclude his business here soon, he'd never make it out of Winsett before nightfall, horse or no. At his feet, the nuns watched the water.

"Mrs. Marchant."

"He wasn't as tall as you are, of course. Happier, though."

Selkirk swung his head toward the woman. She took no notice.

"Of course, why wouldn't he be? He had so much luck in his short life. More than anyone deserves or has any right to expect. The Sacred Heart of Mary Sisters always taught that it was bad luck to consort with the lucky. What do you make of that?"

It took Selkirk several seconds to sort the question, and as he sat, Mrs. Marchant stood abruptly and put her open palm on the window. For a crazy second, just because of the stillness of her posture and the oddly misdirected tilt of her head—toward land, away from the sea—Selkirk wondered if she were blind, like her dolls.

"I guess I've never been around enough luck to have an opinion," Selkirk finally said.

She'd been looking down the coast, but now she turned to him, beaming once more. "The Sisters find you an honest man, sir. They invite you to more tea."

Returning to the bureau with his cup, she refilled it, then sat back down beside him. She'd left the nun she'd had in her lap on the bureau, balancing in the center of a white plate like a tiny ice skater.

"The morning after they set sail," she said, "Luis woke me up." In the window, her eyes reflected against the gray. "He'd gotten better all through the day, and he'd been out all night. He loved to be. I often didn't see him until I came outside to hang the wash or do the chores. But that day, he scratched and whined against the door. I thought he'd fallen or hurt himself again and hurried to let him in. But when I did, he raced straight past me up the stairs. I followed after and found him whimpering against the light there. I was so worried that I didn't even look at the window for the longest time. And when I did…"

All the while, Mrs. Marchant had kept her hands pressed together in the folds of her dress, but now she opened them. Selkirk half-expected a nun to flap free on starfish wings. "So much whiteness, Mr. Selkirk. And yet it was dark. You wouldn't think that would be possible, would you?"

"I've lived by the sea all my life," Selkirk said.

"Well, then. That's what it was like. A wall of white that shed no light. I couldn't even see the water. I had the lamp lit, of course, but all that did was emphasize the difference between *in here* and *out there*."

Selkirk stood. If he were Charlie Marchant, he thought, he would never have left the Convent, as he'd begun to think of this whole place. Not to go to sea. Not even to town. He found himself remembering the letters he'd sent Amalia during his dock-working years. Pathetic, clumsy things. She'd never responded to those, either. Maybe she'd been trying, in her way, to be kind.

"I've often wondered if Luis somehow sensed the ship coming," Mrs. Marchant said. "We'd trained him to bark in the fog, in case a passing captain could hear but not see us. But I think that on this day Luis was just barking at the whiteness.

"The sound was unmistakable when it came. I heard wood splintering. Sails collapsing. A mast smashing into the water. But there wasn't any screaming. And I thought…"

"You thought maybe the crew had escaped to the lifeboats," Selkirk said, when it was clear Mrs. Marchant was not going to finish her sentence.

For the first time in several minutes, Mrs. Marchant turned her gaze on him. "You would make the most marvelous giraffe," she said.

Selkirk stiffened. Was he going to have to carry this poor, gently raving woman out of here? "Mrs. Marchant, it's already late. We need to be starting for town soon."

If she understood what he meant, she gave no sign. "I knew what ship it was." She sank back into her wicker chair, all trace of her smile gone, and crossed her legs. "What other vessel would be out there in the middle of winter? I started screaming, pounding the glass. It didn't take me long to realize they wouldn't have gone to the rowboats. In all likelihood, they'd had no idea where they were. The Kendall boys were experienced seamen, excellent sailors. But that fog had dropped straight out of the heart of the sky, or it had risen from the dead sea bottom, and it was solid as stone.

"And then—as if it were the fogbank itself, and not Charlie's boat, that had run aground on the sandbar out there—all that whiteness just shattered. The whole wall cracked apart into whistling, flying fragments. Just like that, the blizzard blew in. How does that happen, Mr. Selkirk? How does the sea change its mind like that?"

Selkirk didn't answer. But for the first time, he thought he understood why the sailors in the Blubber Pike referred to those teasing, far-off flickers of sun the way they did.

"I rushed downstairs, thinking I'd get the rowboat and haul myself out there and save them. But the waves...they were snarling and snapping all over themselves, and I knew I'd have to wait. My tears were freezing on my face. I was wearing only a dressing gown, and the wind whipped right through me. The door to the lighthouse was banging because I hadn't shut it properly, and I was so full of fury and panic I was ready to start screaming again. I looked out to sea, and all but fell to my knees in gratitude.

"It was there, Mr. Selkirk. I could see the ship. Some of it, anyway. Enough, perhaps. I could just make it out. The prow, part of the foredeck, a stump of mast. I turned around and raced back inside for my clothes.

"Then I ran all the way to town. We never kept a horse here, Charlie didn't like them. The strangest thing was this feeling I kept having, that I'd gotten lost. It was impossible; that path out there was well traveled in those days, and even now, you had no trouble, did you? But I couldn't feel my skin. Or...it was as though I had come *out* of my skin. There was snow and sand flying all around, wind in the dunes. So cold. My Charlie out there. I remember thinking, *This is what the Bruxsa feels like. This is why she torments travelers. This is why she feeds.* You know, at some point, I thought maybe I'd become her."

Selkirk stirred from the daze that had settled over him. "Brucka?"

"*Bruxsa.* It is like...a banshee? Do you know the word? A ghost, but not of anyone. A horrid thing all its own."

Was it his imagination, or had the dark outside deepened toward evening? If he didn't get this finished, neither one of them would make it out of here tonight. "Mrs. Marchant, perhaps we could continue this on the way back to town."

Finally, as though he'd slapped her, Mrs. Marchant blinked. "What?"

"Mrs. Marchant, surely you understand the reason for my coming. We'll send for your things. You don't *have* to leave today, but wouldn't that be easiest? I'll walk with you. I'll make certain—"

"When I finally reached Winsett," Mrs. Marchant said, "I went straight for the first lit window. Selkirk's. The candlemaker. Your uncle."

Selkirk cringed, remembering those hard, overheated hands smashing against the side of his skull. "He was so kind," she said, and his mouth quivered and fell open as she went on.

"He rushed me inside. It was warm in his shop. At the time, it literally felt as though he'd saved my life. Returned me to my body.

I sat by his fire, and he raced all over town through the blizzard and came back with whalers, sailing men. Charlie's father, and the Kendalls' older brother. There were at least fifteen of them. Most set out immediately on horseback for the point. Your uncle wrapped me in two additional sweaters and an overcoat, and he walked all the way back out here with me, telling me it would be all right. By the time we reached the lighthouse, he said, the sailors would already have figured a way to get the boys off that sandbar and home."

To Selkirk, it seemed this woman had reached into his memories and daubed them with colors he knew couldn't have been there. His uncle had been kind to no one. His uncle had hardly spoken except to complete business. The very idea of him using his shop fire to warm somebody, risking himself to rouse the town to some wealthy playboy's rescue...

But of course, by the time Selkirk had come here, the town was well on its way to failing, and his aunt had died in some awful, silent way no one spoke about. Maybe his uncle had been different, before. Or maybe his uncle had been an old lecher, on top of being a drunk.

"By the time we got back here, it was nearly dusk," Mrs. Marchant said. "The older Kendall and four of the sailors had already tried four different times to get the rowboat away from shore and into the waves. They were all tucked inside my house, now, trying to stave off pneumonia.

"'Tomorrow,' one of the sailors told me. 'Tomorrow, please God, if they can just hold on. We'll find a way to them.'

"And right then, Mr. Selkirk. Right as the light went out of that awful day for good, the snow cleared. For one moment. And there they were."

She was almost whispering, now. "It was like a gift. Like a glimpse of him in Heaven. I raced back outside, called out, leapt up and down, we all did. But of course they couldn't hear, and weren't paying attention. They were scrambling all over the deck. I knew right away which was Charlie. He was in the bow, all bundled up in a hat that wasn't his and what looked like three or four coats. I could also see the Kendall boys' hair as they worked amidships. So red, like twin suns burning off the overcast.

"'Bailing,' Charlie's father told me. 'The ship must be taking on water. They're trying to keep her where she is.'"

Mrs. Marchant's voice got even quieter. "I asked how long they could keep doing that. But what I really wondered was how long they'd already been at it. Those poor, beautiful boys.

"Our glimpse lasted two minutes. Maybe even less. I could see new clouds rising behind them. But at the last, just before the snow and the dark obliterated our sight of them, they stopped as one, and turned around. I'm sorry, Mr. Selkirk."

She didn't wipe her face, and there weren't any tears Selkirk could see. She simply sat in her chair, breathing softly.

"I remember the older Kendall, the brother, standing beside me," she finally said, in something close to her normal voice. "He was whispering. '*Aw, come on boys. Get your gear on.*' The Kendalls, you see...they'd removed their coats. And I finally realized what it meant, that I could see their hair. They hadn't bothered with their hats, even though they'd kept at the bailing. Remember, I've been around sailors all my life, Mr. Selkirk. All the men in my family were sailors, long before they came to this country. My father had been whaling here when he sent for us. So I knew what I was seeing."

"And what was that?"

"The Kendalls had given up. Less than 100 yards from shore, they'd given up. Or decided that they weren't going to make it through the night. Either rescue would come before dawn, or it would no longer matter. The ship would not hold. Or the cold would overwhelm them. So they were hastening the end, one way or another.

"But not Charlie. Not my Charlie. He didn't jump in the air. He just slumped against the railing. But I know he saw me, Mr. Selkirk. I could *feel* his gaze. Even at that distance. I could always feel his gaze. Then the snow came back. And night fell.

"The next time we saw them, they were in the rigging."

Silently, Selkirk gave up the idea of escaping Winsett until morning. The network of functioning lights and functional keepers the Service had been toiling so hard to establish could wait one more winter evening.

"This was midday, the second day. That storm was a freak of nature. Or perhaps not natural at all. How can that much wind blow a storm nowhere? It was as though the blizzard itself had locked jaws on those boys—on my boy—and would not let go. The men who weren't already wracked by coughs and fever made another five attempts with the rowboat, and never got more than a few feet from shore. The ice in the air was like arrows raining down.

"Not long after the last attempt, when almost everyone was indoors and I was rushing about making tea and caring for the sick and trying to shush Luis, who had been barking since dawn, I heard Charlie's father yell and hurried outside.

"I'd never seen light like that, Mr. Selkirk, and I haven't since. Neither snow nor wind had eased one bit, and the clouds hadn't lifted. But there was the ship again, and there were our boys. Up in the ropes, now. The Kendalls had their hats back on and their coats around them. They were nestled together with their arms through the lines. Charlie had gone even higher, crouching by himself, looking down at the brothers or maybe the deck. I hoped they were talking to each other, or singing, anything to keep their spirits up and their breath in them. Because the ship…. Have you ever seen quicksand, Mr. Selkirk? It was almost like that, the way the whole thing was sinking, little by steady little. This glimpse lasted a minute, maybe less. But in that time, the hull dropped what looked like another full foot underwater. And that was the only thing we saw move."

"I don't understand," Selkirk said. "The sandbar was right there. It's what they hit, right? Or the rocks right around it? Why not just climb down?"

"If they'd so much as put their feet in that water, after all they'd been exposed to, they would have frozen on the spot. All they could do was cling to the ropes.

"So they clung. The last healthy men came out behind Charlie's father and me to watch. And somehow, just the clear sight of the ship out there inspired us all. Everyone got angry and active again.

"We actually got close once, just at dark. The snow hadn't cleared, but the wind had eased. The sickest men, including the older Kendall boy, had been run back to town on horseback, and we hoped other Winsett whalers might be rigging up a brig in the harbor to try reaching Charlie's ship from the sea-side, rather than from land, the moment the weather permitted. I kept thinking I'd heard new sounds out there, caught a glimpse of the mast of a rescue vessel. But of course it was too soon, and we couldn't really hear or see anything but the storm, anyway. And in the midst of another round of crazy, useless running about, Charlie's father grabbed my wrist and whirled me around to face the water and said, 'Stop. Listen.'

"And I understood finally that I heard nothing. Sweet, beautiful nothing. The wind had been in my ears so long, I hadn't noticed its absence. Right away I imagined that I should be able to hear Charlie and the Kendalls through the quiet. Before anyone could stop me, I was racing for the shore, my feet flying into the frozen water and my dress freezing against my legs, but I could hardly feel it. I was already so cold, so numb. We all were. I started screaming my husband's name. It was too shadowy and snowy to see. But I went right on screaming, and everyone else on our little beach held still.

"But I got no answer. If it weren't for the swirling around my feet, I might have thought even the water had had its voice sucked from it.

"And then."

Finally, for the first time, Mrs. Marchant's voice broke. In a horrible way, Selkirk realized he envied her this experience. No single hour, let alone day, had ever impressed itself on him the way these days had on her, except perhaps for those few fleeting, sleet-drenched moments with Amalia. And those hardly counted, somehow.

When Mrs. Marchant continued, the quaver had gone, as though she'd swallowed it. "It was to be the last time I heard his real voice, Mr. Selkirk. I think I already knew that. And when I remember it now, I'm not even certain I really did hear it. How could I have? It was a croak, barely even a whisper. But it was Charlie's voice. I'd still swear to that, in spite of everything, even though he said just the one word. '*Hurry*.'

"The last two remaining men from Winsett needed no further encouragement. In an instant, they had the rowboat in the water. Charlie's father and I shoved them off while they pulled with all their might against the crush of the surf. For a minute, no more, they hung up in that same spot that had devilled all our efforts for the past 36 hours, caught in waves that beat them back and back. Then they just sprung free. All of a sudden, they were in open water, heaving with all their might toward the sandbar. We were too exhausted to clap or cheer. But my heart leapt so hard in my chest I thought it might break my ribs.

"As soon as they were twenty feet from shore, we lost sight of them, and later, they said all they saw was blackness and water and snow, so none of us knows how close they actually got. They were gone six, maybe seven minutes. Then, as if a dike had collapsed, sound came rushing over us. The wind roared in and brought a new, hard sleet. There was a last, terrible pause that none of us mistook for calm. The water had simply risen up, you see, Mr. Selkirk. It lifted our rescue rowboat in one giant black wave and hurled it halfway up the beach. The two men in the boat got slammed to the sand. Fortunately—miraculously, really—the wave hadn't crested until it was nearly on top of the shore, so neither man drowned. One broke both wrists, the other his nose and teeth. Meanwhile, the water poured up the beach, soaked us all, and retreated as instantaneously as it had come."

For the first time, Selkirk realized that the story he was hearing no longer quite matched the one Amalia had told him. Even more startling, Amalia's had been less cruel. In Amalia's version, no rescues had been attempted because none had been possible. No real hope had ever emerged. The ship had simply slid off the sandbar, and all aboard had drowned.

"Waves don't simply rise up," he said.

Mrs. Marchant tilted her head. "No? My father used to come home from half a year at sea and tell us stories. Waves riding the ghost of a wind two years gone and two thousand leagues distant, roaming alone like great, rogue beasts. Not an uncommon occurrence on the open ocean."

"But this isn't the open ocean."

"And you think the ocean knows, or cares? Though I will admit to you, Mr. Selkirk. At the time, it seemed like the sea just didn't want us out there.

"By now, the only two healthy people at Cape Roby Point were Charlie's father and me. And when that new sleet kept coming and coming...well. We didn't talk about it. We made our wounded rowers as comfortable as we could by the fire on the rugs inside. Then we set about washing bedding, setting out candles. I began making this little Sister here—" as she spoke, she toed the doll with the white bandeau, which leaned against her feet "—to keep Charlie company in his coffin. Although both of us knew, I'm sure, that we weren't even likely to get the bodies back.

"My God, the sounds of that night. I can still hear the sleet drumming on the roof. The wind around the tower. All I could think about was Charlie out there, clinging to the ropes for hope of reaching me. I knew he would be gone by morning. Around two A.M., Charlie's father fell asleep leaning against a wall, and I eased him into a chair and sank down on the floor beside him. I must have been so exhausted that I slept, too, without meaning to, right there at his feet.

"And when I woke..."

The Kendalls, Selkirk thought, as he watched the woman purse her mouth and hold still. Had he known them? It seemed to him he'd at least known who they were. At that time, though, he'd had eyes only for Amalia.

"When I woke," Mrs. Marchant murmured, "there was sunlight. I didn't wait to make sense of what I was seeing. I didn't think about what I'd find. I didn't wake Charlie's father, but he came roaring after me as I sprinted from the house.

"We didn't even know if our rowboat would float. We made straight for it anyway. I didn't look at the sandbar. Do you find that strange? I didn't want to see. Not yet. I looked at the dunes, and they were gold, Mr. Selkirk. With the blown grass and seaweed and debris strewn all over them, they looked newly born, wanting only their mother to lick them clean.

"The rowboat had landed on its side. The wood had begun to split in the bow, but Charlie's father thought it would hold. Anyway, it was all we had, our last chance. We righted it and dragged it to the water, which was like glass. Absolutely flat, barely rolling over to touch the beach. Charlie's father wasn't waiting for me. He'd already got into the boat and begun to pull. But when I caught the back and dragged myself in, he held position just long enough. Then he started rowing for all he was worth.

"For a few seconds longer, I kept my head down. I wanted to pray, but I couldn't. My mother was a Catholic, and we'd worked for the Sacred Heart Sisters, as I told you. But I was so tired. So in love, Mr. Selkirk. And maybe I never believed, anyway. So when I closed my eyes, I heard only the seagulls squealing around, and no prayer came to me. I just wanted Charlie back. Finally, I lifted my head.

"I didn't gasp, or cry out. I don't think I even felt anything.

"First off, there were only two of them. The highest was Charlie. He'd climbed almost to the very top of what was left of the main mast, which had tilted over so far that it couldn't have been more than twenty-five feet above the water. Even with that overcoat engulfing him and the hat pulled all the way down over his ears, I could tell by the arms and legs snarled in the rigging that it was him.

"'Is he moving, girl?' Charlie's father asked, and I realized he hadn't been able to bring himself to look, either. We lurched closer.

"Then I did gasp, Mr. Selkirk. Just once. Because he *was* moving. Or I thought he was. He seemed to be settling…resettling…I can't explain it. He was winding his arms and legs through the ropes, like a child trying to fit into a hiding place as you come for him. As if he'd just gotten back to that spot. Or maybe the movement was wind. Even now, I don't know.

"Charlie's father swore at me and snarled his question again. When I didn't answer, he turned around. 'Lord Jesus,' I heard him say. After that, he put his head down and rowed. And I kept my eyes on Charlie, and the empty blue sky beyond him. Anywhere but down the mast, where the other Kendall boy hung.

"By his ankles, Mr. Selkirk. His ankles, and nothing more. God only knows what held him there. The wind had torn his clothes right off him. He had his eyes and his mouth open. He looked so pale, so thin, nothing like he had in life. His body had red slashes all over it, as though the storm had literally tried to rip him open.

"Charlie's father gave one last heave, and our little boat knocked against the last showing bit of the Kendalls' ship's hull. The masts above us groaned, and I thought the whole thing was going to crash down on top of us. Charlie's father tried to wedge an oar in the wood, get us in close, and finally he just rowed around the ship and ran us aground on the sandbar. I leapt out after him, thinking I should be the one to climb the mast. I was lighter, less likely to sink the whole thing once and for all. Our home, our lighthouse, was so close it seemed I could have waded over and grabbed it. I probably could have. I leaned back, looked up again, and this time I was certain I saw Charlie move.

"His father saw it, too, and he started screaming. He wasn't even making words, but I was. I had my arms wide open, and I was calling my husband. 'Come down. Come home, my love.' I saw his arms disentangle themselves, his legs slide free. The ship sagged beneath him. If he so much as touched that water, I thought, it would be too much. The cold would have him at the last. He halted, and his father stopped screaming, and I went silent.

He hung there so long I thought he'd died after all, now that he'd heard our voices one last time. Then, hand over hand, so painfully slowly, like a spider crawling down a web, he began to edge upside-down over the ropes. He reached the Kendall boy's poor, naked body and bumped it with his hip. It swung out and back, out and back. Charlie never even looked, and he didn't slow or alter his path. He kept coming.

"I don't even remember how he got over the rail. As he reached the deck, he disappeared a moment from our sight. We were trying to figure how to get up there to him. Then he just climbed over the edge and fell to the sand at our feet. The momentum from his body seemed to give the wreck a final push, or it was simply ready to go; it slid off the sandbar into the water and sank, taking the Kendall boy's body with it.

"The effort of getting down had taken everything Charlie had. His eyes were closed. His breaths were shallow, and he didn't respond when we shook him. So Charlie's father lifted him and dropped him in the rowboat. I hopped in the bow with my back to the shore, and Charlie's father began to pull desperately for the mainland. I was sitting calf-deep in water, cradling my husband's head facedown in my lap. I stroked his cheeks, and they were so cold. Impossibly cold, and bristly, and hard. Like rock. I was willing all the heat I had left into my fingers, and I was cooing like a dove. Charlie's father had his back to us, pulling for everything he was worth. He never turned around. And so he didn't…"

Once more, Mrs. Marchant's voice trailed away. Out the filthy windows, in the gray that had definitely darkened into full-blown dusk now, Selkirk could see a single trail of yellow-red, right at the horizon, like the glimpse of eye underneath a cat's closed lid. Tomorrow the weather would clear. And he would be gone, on his way home. Maybe he would stay there this time. Find somebody he didn't have to pay to keep him company.

"It's a brave thing you've done, Mrs. Marchant," he said, and before he could think what he was doing, he slid forward and took her chilly hand in his. He meant nothing by it but comfort, and was surprised to discover the sweet, transitory sadness of another person's fingers curled in his. A devil's smile of a feeling, if ever there was one. "He was a good man, your husband. You have mourned him properly and well."

"Just a boy," she whispered.

"A good boy, then. And he loved you. You have paid him the tribute he deserved, and more. And now it's time to do him the honor of living again. Come back to town. I'll see you somewhere safe and warm. I'll see you there myself, if you'll let me."

Very slowly, without removing her fingers, Mrs. Marchant raised her eyes to his, and her mouth came open. "You...you silly man. You think.... But you said you knew the story."

Confused, Selkirk squeezed her hand. "I know it now."

"You believe I have stayed here, cut off from all that is good in the world, shut up like an abbess all these years with my Sisters and my memories, for love? For grief?"

Now Selkirk let go, watching as Mrs. Marchant's hand fluttered before settling in her lap like a blown leaf. "There's no crime in that, surely. But now—"

"I've always wondered how the rowboat flipped," she said, in a completely new, flat voice devoid of all her half-sung tones, as he stuttered to silence. "All the times I've gone through it and over it, and I can't get it straight. I can't see how it happened."

Unsure what to do with his hands, Selkirk finally settled them on his knees. "The rowboat?"

"Dead calm. There was no rogue wave this time. We were twenty yards from shore. Less. We could have hopped out and walked. I was still cooing. Still stroking my husband's cheeks. But I knew already. And I think his father knew, too. Charlie had died before we even got him in the boat. He wasn't breathing. Wasn't moving. He hadn't during the whole, silent trip back to shore. I turned toward land to see exactly how close we were. And just like that I was in the water.

"If you had three men and were trying, you couldn't flip a boat that quickly. One of the oars banged me on the head. I don't know if it was that or the cold that stunned me. But I couldn't think.

For a second, I had no idea which way was up, even in three feet of water, and then my feet found bottom and I stood and staggered toward shore. The oar had caught me right on the scalp and a stream of blood kept pouring into my eyes. I wasn't thinking about Charlie. I wasn't thinking anything except that I needed to be out of the cold before I became it. I could feel it in my blood. I got to the beach, collapsed in the sun, remembered where I was and what I'd been doing, and spun around.

"There was the boat, floating right-side up, as though it hadn't flipped at all. Oars neatly shipped, like arms folded across a chest. Water still as a lagoon beneath it. And neither my husband nor his father *anywhere*.

"I almost laughed. It was impossible. Ridiculous. So cruel, after everything else. I didn't scream. I waited, scanning the water, ready to lunge in and save Charlie's dad if I could only see him. But there was nothing. No trace. I sat down and stared at the horizon and didn't weep. It seemed perfectly possible that I might freeze to death right there, completing the carnage. I even opened the throat of my dress, thinking of the Kendall boys shedding their coats that first day. That's what I was doing when Charlie crawled out of the water."

Selkirk stood up. "But you said—"

"He'd lost his hat. And his coat had come open. He crawled right up the beach, sidewise, like a crab. Just the way he had down the rigging. Of course, my arms opened to him, and the cold dove down my dress. I was laughing, Mr. Selkirk. Weeping and laughing and cooing, and his head swung up, and I saw."

With a single, determined wriggle of her shoulders, Mrs. Marchant went completely still. She didn't speak again for several minutes. Helpless, Selkirk sat back down.

"The only question I had in the end, Mr. Selkirk, was *when* it had happened."

For no reason he could name, Selkirk experienced a flash of Amalia's cruel, haunted face, and tried for the thousandth time to imagine where she'd gone. Then he thought of the dead town behind him, the debris disappearing piece by piece and bone by bone into the dunes, his aunt's silent death. His uncle. He'd never made any effort to determine what had happened to his uncle after Amalia vanished.

"I still think about the Kendall boys, you know," Mrs. Marchant murmured. "Every day. The one suspended in the ropes, exposed like that, all torn up. And the one that disappeared. Do you think he jumped to get away, Mr. Selkirk? I think he might have. I would have."

"What on earth are you—"

"Even the dead's eyes reflect light," she said, turning her bright and living ones on him. "Did you know that? But Charlie's eyes....Of course, it wasn't really Charlie anymore, but..."

Selkirk almost leapt to his feet again, wanted to, wished he could hurtle downstairs, flee into the dusk. "What do you mean?"

For answer, Mrs. Marchant cocked her head at him, and a wisp of a smile hovered over her mouth and evaporated. "What do I mean? How do I know? Was it a ghost? Do you know how many hundreds of sailors have died within five miles of this point? Surely one or two of them might have been angry about it."

"Are you actually saying—"

"Or maybe that's silly. Maybe it was the sea. Something that lives in it. I can't tell you. What I can tell you is that there was *no Charlie* in the face before me, Mr. Selkirk. None. I had no doubt. No question. My only hope was that whatever it was had come for him after he was already gone, the way a hermit crab climbs inside a shell. Please God, if there is such a creature, let it be the wind and the cold that took my husband."

Staggering upright, Selkirk shook his head. "You said he was dead."

"So he was."

"You were mistaken."

"It killed the Kendall boy, Mr. Selkirk. It crawled down and tore him to shreds. I'm fairly certain it killed its own father as well. Charlie's father, I mean. Luis took one look at him and vanished into the dunes. I never saw the dog again."

"Of course it was him. You're not yourself, Mrs. Marchant. All these years alone. . . . It spared you, didn't it? Didn't he?"

Mrs. Marchant smiled one more time and broke down weeping, silently. "It had just eaten," she whispered. "Or whatever it is it does. Or maybe I had just lost my last loved ones, and stank of the saltwater, had no heat left in my body, and it thought I was *like* it. One of it."

"Listen," Selkirk said, and on impulse he dropped to one knee and took her hands once more. God, but they were cold. So many years in this cold, with this weight on her shoulders. "That day was so full of tragedy. Whatever you think you..."

Very slowly, Selkirk stopped. His mind retreated down the stairs, out the lighthouse door to the mainland, over the disappearing path he'd walked between the dunes, and all the way back into Winsett. He saw anew the shuttered boarding houses and empty taverns. He saw the street where his uncle's cabin had been. What had happened to his uncle? His aunt? *Amalia?* Where had they gone? Just how long had it taken Winsett to die? His mind scrambled farther out of town, up the track he had taken, between the discarded pans and decaying whale bones toward the other silent, deserted towns all along this blasted section of the Cape. *Where were all these people?*

"Mrs. Marchant," he whispered, his hands tightening around hers, having finally understood why she had shut herself up in this tower. What she thought was happening out there. "Mrs. Marchant, please. Where is Charlie now?"

She stood, then, and twined one gentle finger through the tops of his curls as she wiped at her tears. The gesture felt dispassionate, almost maternal, something a mother might do to a son who has just awoken. He looked up and found her gazing again, not out to sea but over the dunes at the dark streaming inland. *Had she actually seen him since? Seen* it? *Prowling the dunes like a wolf, with bones in its mouth...*

"It's going to get even colder," she said. "I'll put the kettle on."

Transitway

"Is there any need to explain why
fear eats the soul of Los Angeles?"
—Mike Davis

On the first day of his retirement, Ferdinand Fernandez awoke to banging on his front door. For a few, fuzzy moments, the sound bewildered him. He couldn't remember the last time he'd actually heard it. Rolling over, he dropped his hand onto the empty pillow beside him, momentarily wondered at the ghost of heat he imagined he felt there, then forgot it as whoever was outside banged again.

"Coming," Ferdinand mumbled, digging into the pile of clean but unfolded Hawaiian shirts he never bothered to return to his single chest of drawers. The one he pulled up was mostly blue, with swordfish leaping across it. Struggling into that and a pair of shorts, he stood up barefoot on his futon, feeling his gut drop onto his hipbones like some exhausted geriatric leaning over a seawall, and caught sight of the clock.

10:30.

The panic that seized him wasn't entirely surprising. He'd felt it buzzing around in his dreams all night. And it had probably been thirty years since he'd slept this long. This time, the banging on the door rattled his living room clock off the wall.

"Goddamnit," Ferdinand barked, though half-heartedly. As he stepped across the warped hardwood floor of his bungalow in his bare feet, he decided it wouldn't be the worst thing to see another human being's face this morning. Any human being's. After all, today—and pretty much every day, from now on—there would be no one, anywhere, waiting for him.

Throwing open the door, he blinked against the blinding L.A. sunlight, and Q shoved him backward and strolled in, brandishing a black satchel. His shined two-toned shoes clopped, as though they had taps attached. Knowing Q, Ferdinand thought, they just might.

"Out the way, freed slave coming through," Q said, bounding straight across the living room, through the kitchen toward the unused back hallway and the bungalow's other room.

For the second time that morning, panic flared in Ferdinand's chest. "Where the hell are you going?"

At the sound of his voice, Q stopped dead, one foot still in the kitchen, the other poised above the scraggly tan carpeting of the hall. When he turned around, he was wearing the surprised smile that had, all by itself, made him a better teacher than Ferdinand, and an exceptionally long-lived department chair. There was something endearing about someone so completely in charge being that willing, and that often, to be caught off guard.

"No idea," he said. "Seems like last time I was here, we..."

"Last time?" Ferdinand blinked, rubbed at the sleep in his eyes and wound up smearing sweat there instead. "When was that, exactly?"

By now, Q had recovered, become Q again. "Right 'round the last time you invited me, F-Squared."

Ferdinand winced, although he knew Q hadn't meant any insult. The nickname had been pasted to him by a recent class of students, and was a term of affectionate mockery since, other than P.E., his courses had become probably the hardest to fail in all of Florence Normandie High School. He hadn't meant to go soft. He'd just lost the point, somewhere, of telling these particular kids, facing their particular choices, that they sucked at communicating.

For a long breath, the two men stared at each other. Outside, the air Q had disturbed filled again with its more familiar sound: the gush and snarl of traffic pouring over the 110 freeway just down the block like the morning tide. Ferdinand eyed his boss—ex-boss—and felt a surge of startling and powerful gratitude. For thirty-four years, going to work had been better than it might have been because he got to spend at least twenty or so minutes of his time each day with this man.

Except that looking at Q now, it seemed Ferdinand hadn't really seen him for years. *When, exactly, had Q gotten old?* Well into his fifties, Q had kept his 'fro flying—*"Springy as a trampoline, soft as your butt"*—but sometime recently he'd shaved it down, and now all he had atop his knobby black skull were outcroppings of charcoal fuzz, like dead moss on a boulder. What had been Q's barrel chest was now a barrel all the way to his hips, and it swung when he walked.

"What?" Q snapped.

Ferdinand gestured at the black satchel. "That's your idea for our first day of retirement? Bowling?"

Q unzipped the satchel with a flourish, then drew out the strobe ball that had hung over his desk for three decades. He laid that on Ferdinand's white, round, plastic kitchen table, then pulled out eight bottles of Corona and set those ceremoniously next to the ball before flinging the bag away.

"Not your real uncle, praise the Lord," Ferdinand murmured, then blinked as Q straightened up, mouth flat.

"What?"

"I don't know." Ferdinand's breath felt furry and uncomfortable in his mouth. From too much sleep, perhaps. "Didn't I used to say that to you? Or some student?"

Q shrugged, settled back into his habitual, hip-cocked, preening posture. "Well, I ain't your uncle. I'm your daddy." And he waved at the beer and the strobe. "You imagine how boring this year's end-of-term wine-and-whine faculty meeting's going to be without me and my stuff?"

"I'm still trying to get over how boring they were *with* your stuff."

Q grinned. "What's for breakfast, fellow free man?"

While Ferdinand got bowls down from his cabinet for cereal,

Q wandered again toward the hallway that led to the back room. It made Ferdinand nervous. *God, when was the last time even he'd been back there? Guest* room, that's what he'd called it. *Hadn't he?* Stupid conceit. By the time he'd finally managed to save enough scraps from twenty-six years of teaching paychecks to put a down payment on this place, his parents had been long dead, and his sisters had moved to Fullerton with their families, which was just far enough away for them to visit less often, but not far enough for them to sleep over. Except for Q, his school colleagues had stayed colleagues, not friends, and if Q ever did sleep over, it would be face down wherever the last Corona had left him, not in a bed. Right this second, Ferdinand couldn't even remember if there *was* a bed in that room. Whatever furniture there was in there, the termites and dust must have long since claimed it.

Pouring oat bran and milk into the bowls, Ferdinand let his eyes close for just a moment. People had warned him about the first hours of retirement. He'd told them they were crazy, it wouldn't be like that for him. From outside, sluicing through walls honeycombed with termite nests he couldn't afford to eradicate, came the gush of freeway noise. There should have been other sounds out there, too. Had been, once. The *blatt* and *thud* from some souped-up ride stereo, say, or the sound of neighborhood kids woofing at each other's sisters. But his neighborhood had gone silent of late. Or else the freeway had overflowed its banks and drowned out everything else.

He turned, and Q scowled.

"What is that? Bran? I bring you my strobe, you offer me *fiber?*" Sweeping both bowls out of Ferdinand's hands, Q flipped them upside down into the sink. "Where the eggs?"

He didn't wait for Ferdinand to point to the refrigerator before popping it open. "Good. Where the peppers? You people always have peppers." He found those, too, piled in the vegetable drawer. "Okey-dokey. Now. Dance."

And all at once, Ferdinand realized it was all true. There would be no more Back-to-School night. No more "Wait, you teach *English*?" No more beautiful, still-hopeful faces disappearing mid-semester into their South Central lives and never coming back. No more F-Squared. No more no-flip-flops days. Dropping into a pose he could only hope was as gleeful as he felt, he launched himself into the *Macarena*.

"That's my boy." Q started cracking eggs, but Ferdinand completed a circle and bumped him out of the way, snatching up a knife and beginning to chop at the *jalapenos*.

"These eggs might make you weep," he said.

"Your dancing's going to make me weep," said Q.

Several seconds went by before Ferdinand realized his friend had neither returned to the table nor cracked the remaining eggs. Instead, he was staring into the sink.

"I gave you that," he said slowly, reached down, and lifted the bowl. It was white, with a picture of an apple-cheeked Red Riding Hood and a particularly sleazy, slobbering gray wolf under a red-checked bedcover painted on the bottom.

Ferdinand nodded. "Revenge, I think. For that..." *Skeleton piñata? Was that right? What had started them trading gifts like that?*

Eventually, Q shrugged. "Still no reason to put bran in it."

"Sorry. Go sit."

Ferdinand wound up folding in so many peppers that the eggs turned sticky green-brown, the color of the palm fronds that somehow sucked nourishment from between the particulates in the L.A. air and kept growing alongside every deserted sidewalk and choked roadway. When presented with his plate, Q nodded his approval absently, flooded his entire plate with Tabasco sauce, then gulped it all down in silence.

From his own seat, Ferdinand stared past his friend, through the strings of dust drifting in the air like lines on an old TV set, into his living room. There was his old brown vinyl couch, the cushion on one side collapsed like an exhausted lung. Past the couch stood the matching free-standing bookshelves he'd bought from IKEA a few years back on a splurge, then accidentally assembled upside down so that the rough sides pointed out. Books crammed every available inch of those shelves, and piled up on the floor, too. He spent the great majority of his non-school time in there, so the dust all over everything surprised him.

Cracking open a Corona, Q fished a lime out of a baggie he kept in his shirt pocket, squeezed some into the beer, and drank half of it in a single draft. Then he sighed, returned the lime and baggie to his pocket, and crossed his ankles beneath the table. "Okay. What's it going to be, Ferd? What we gonna do with all this *time*? Santa Anita, bet us some ponies?"

"Too poor." Ferdinand initially waved off the new bottle Q offered him, then took it after Q popped it open with his thumbnail, the way he always did.

"How 'bout over to Swinger's, case us some ladies?"

Ferdinand smiled. "Too tired of people. And we're too fat."

"Plus, you dance funny. Okay, your turn."

"Clifton's," Ferdinand said.

Immediately, Q slapped the table with his open palm and laughed. "Hot damn. Clifton's, for some *roast* beef."

"And a pudding."

"Pudding, too."

"Eat in the trees."

Q laughed again. "Remember that time there, with the waterfall, when Moe—"

"Milt," Ferdinand corrected, and Q stopped.

Both men stared at each other. For the third or fourth time that morning, queasiness bubbled in Ferdinand's stomach. Finally, Q pushed a breath between his teeth.

"Milt," he said, as if the word were foreign, brand new to him.

"Pretty sure. Can't remember anything else about him, but that was his name."

"Just a kid."

"Field trip, maybe."

"Must have been."

After another few seconds of looking at each other, then down at the table, Ferdinand got up and put the dishes in the sink. The idea of Clifton's Cafeteria really did seem right. They'd tuck themselves at one of the tables by the indoor waterfall, beneath the giant fake trees, then sit for hours and watch Hollywood hustlers work the ground floor and get in arguments with Grand Market wheelchair thieves, while retro Zoot Suit thugs swung pocket watches and cribbed betting tips from old ladies stuffing themselves with French dips and dripping sauce all over their Santa Anita racing forms. Best people-watching in Los Angeles.

"Hey, Q. After Clifton's, how about the main library? Check out some books we finally have time to read."

"Just as long as none of them's Flecker," Q barked, and leapt to his feet to toss his second empty Corona into Ferdinand's recycle bag.

This time, Ferdinand's smile didn't make him nauseous. Just wistful. Teaching in an academic system that had ditched Dickens, Twain, Dickinson, Hurston, Faulkner, Hughes, and Wright as either too difficult for the students or irrelevant to their lives, Ferdinand had devoted a week or more, over thirty-plus years of objections from department chairs and district "curriculum advisors," to *The Golden Journey to Samarkind.* Partially, this was because there were always one or two kids, each year, who responded to poems about getting *somewhere else.* Partially, it was because not one of the parents who'd actually turned up for Back-to-School night had heard of Flecker, a fact Ferdinand never failed to enjoy, since the parents almost invariably asked if he weren't the Spanish teacher.

Mostly, though, Ferdinand had stuck to Flecker because that's what his father had read by campfire or starlight during his frozen three-week crawl up the cactus-strewn wastes of El Camino del Diablo over the border into Great Depression Arizona in 1938.

"For lust of knowing what should not be known," he found himself mouthing, for the thousandth time in his life. *"For lust of knowing what should not be known."* His students would forget him, every one. But in their most haunted hours—on their

wedding night, maybe, or the day they fled town, or the eve of their very first gangbang—one or two would inexplicably murmur the forlorn phrases of a twilight-of-the-Empire British twit who'd dreamed hard and died young. A pathetic legacy, maybe. But a legacy, nevertheless.

"Move your Fleckered ass, and let's roll," said Q, and Ferdinand went.

Moments later, humming the *Macarena* to himself as Q downed yet another beer, Ferdinand led the way onto the cracked and weedy driveway to his 1974 Vega, shoved his key through the channel he'd made in the rust on the doorlock, and popped the doors.

"Sweet *Jesus*, get the air on," Q moaned as he settled onto the scalding, split vinyl.

"Air?" Ferdinand grinned. "They make 'em with air, now?" He jammed the key in the ignition and turned it.

The car didn't kick or even cough. It just sat. The grin stayed stuck to Ferdinand's face. This was only right, after all. Only fair. Every year, usually by dark on the first night of Christmas break, he came down with the flu he'd held off all fall, and stayed sick most of the vacation. Like his body, the Vega had apparently known precisely when it was okay, at long last, to go ahead and give out.

For a few seconds, Ferdinand sat and baked in the morning sunlight, stroking the cracking dashboard as though it were the muzzle of a horse. A dead horse. Then he said, "Think maybe we should take your car."

Q grunted. "Walked."

Ferdinand turned his head in surprise. "All the way from..." *Where did Q live again? He knew, of course he knew, he'd gone there all the time when...*

"Wanted to see and hear people, you know? Felt weird getting up this morning, knowing no one's waiting."

Ferdinand nodded.

"Of course, L.A. being the great throbbing nowhere it has always been, I hardly saw anyone anyway."

"City of cars."

"Hardly even saw those. Had to trot onto a freeway overpass just to make sure everyone was still out there."

Sighing, Ferdinand waved a hand toward the window and the noise roaring up the 110. "Pretty sure they're still out there."

"Yeah, but where the hell are they going? Not *my* neighborhood."

The air in the car seared Ferdinand's lungs, seemed to seal his skin like paint. Nudging the door open, he climbed out, wanting to be away from Q for just a moment, and wandered to the edge of his driveway to stare at the row of stunted trees lining his street.

This was the scariest thing about bad L.A., he thought. Not a single moving car in sight. No faces at windows, no summer vacation kids on bicycles. But with the sunlight pouring honey on the palm trees and carefully kept rooftops and porches, and the purple flowers on the jacarandas swinging like little bells in the morning breeze, and that dry, delicious heat seeping up from the desert sand still stirring under all that concrete, you could so easily trick yourself into mistaking this place for some seaside Spanish town at siesta.

Just try not to notice the bars latticed over the miniature square windows of each stucco-and-cedar bungalow. Try not to acknowledge the way those bungalows hunch too close together on their tiny, ice-plant-choked lots like circled wagons. This particular low-income development had gone up in the 1940s, but despite its age, and like most southern California neighborhoods—rich or poor, grafted onto the hillsides or welded into the desert—the buildings all looked as though they could be coupled together and rolled off the landscape in a single afternoon.

Even so, Q's description of his morning walk nagged at Ferdinand. Had his neighborhood always been *this* quiet? Where were the earthquake tremors of hip-hop bass as the local teens threw open their car doors and sat on their driveways to smoke pot and stare at each other? Where were the women, older mostly, heads wrapped in scarves despite the heat, wheeling shopping carts to the convenience store, glaring their defiance at each passing gaggle of driveway boys?

Behind him, Ferdinand heard a single, hollow *thunk*. For no reason, the sound horrified him, made him afraid to turn around. His sweaty hands clenched at his sides. With a grunt, he forced himself to look back.

Q stood three steps out onto the square patch of dead, petrified grass that passed for Ferdinand's front yard. In one huge fist, he was holding the handle of a yellow Wiffle bat. When he saw Ferdinand looking, he *thunked* the barrel again against the ground.

"This a Wiffle bat in my hands, or am I just happy to see you?" Q said.

Ferdinand realized his own hands had stayed clenched. And deep in his throat, something was squeezing.

"Leave that," he croaked.

"What, here?"

"Where you found it."

"Found it right here, what the hell's the matter with you?"

"Put it back."

Raising a single eyebrow, Q ran a hand through his scraggle of hair. Then, with exaggerated pomp, he knelt and laid the bat gently in the dead grass. As Ferdinand watched, the bat seemed to lift slightly, then settle, like a bottle with a message in it washing out to sea. Abruptly, he stepped forward and picked it up himself.

The plastic had long since mottled and cracked, and a faint, fetid odor wafted out of a pinhole in the top. Ferdinand swung the bat once, in slow motion, and whatever it was in his throat constricted again. *Milt. Not your real uncle. My, Q, what big hair you have...*

"Goddamn," Q said. "Retirement's gone and made you wack."

"Think it was you that did that," Ferdinand mumbled.

"Used to play a lot, you know. Wiffle."

"I know."

"You do?"

Glancing up, Ferdinand was startled by the look on his friend's face. Mouth puckered, eyes glazed, turned inward. Pretty much like his own look, he suspected. "We've known each other a long time," he said, though he somehow thought he'd meant to say something else. He tapped the barrel into the grass.

What was it about that sound? Maybe just that there wasn't enough of it. It barely stirred the air, like footsteps on an unmiked soundstage. Silently, he cursed the Vega. He didn't want to be home anymore. He felt invisible enough already.

And then, all at once, as though someone had kicked a volume switch, noise poured into his ears. That permanent freeway roar, like the world's largest summer fan except it ran all year and made everything hotter instead of cooler, less bearable instead of more, and was so omnipresent he'd stopped noticing it half the time. Turning to Q again, he felt at least a semblance of a smile creep back over his mouth.

"Got an idea."

"This your first time?"

"Transitway," Ferdinand said.

Slowly, as though awakening from a deep sleep, Q shivered and glanced toward the street. "What about it?"

"Riding it, what do you think?" Ferdinand felt cramping in his fingers, then all the way up his arms. The sensation was painful, and also weirdly reassuring. *He was still part of the world. Could go where people were, be a resident of the city, even if everyone in it had already forgotten he was there.* "Thought you wanted to go to Clifton's."

"*Before* I die," Q said. "Thought maybe I'd put off my murder until just a few days after my retirement."

But Ferdinand could see, by the way Q was shifting his weight back and forth and shaking his head, that the idea intrigued him, too. "Aw, come on. You, the caller of everyone else's bullshit. Who do you know who's even ridden the Transitway?"

"We are talking about the Transitway, as in the bus line that runs up the damn 110, right? As in right *on* the 110? The one where people finally just hurl themselves off the bus stop benches into traffic 'cause they're already deaf from cars screaming by and burnt to death 'cause there ain't no shade and they've stopped breathing anyway because the carbon monoxide ate their lungs. *That* Transitway?"

"Again," said Ferdinand, closing his weary eyes and feeling further from smiling than he usually did when Q started ranting. "Who do you know who's ever ridden it?"

"Whoever it was told me there are whole gangs shooting up together in the stairwells. Using the homeless people and anyone else they find down there as dinner tables."

"Hell, they're probably using them as dinner," Ferdinand said, and now he did start to smile.

"That's somewhere south of funny."

Ferdinand had heard the stories, too. "Look, what I heard, there's *no one* down there. City poured all that money into it, and people won't even go on the thing. 10,000 riders a day, they were expecting. I saw an article not too long ago that said they get less than 500."

"Wonder if that's because they built the stations *right on the fucking freeway*. We'll be waiting—probably two hours, given traffic and the frequency of buses our neighborhoods have always been granted—on a concrete island in dead sunlight or under some overpass where only the passing cars can see us get our guts ripped out, if anyone who happens to be around is in a gut-ripping mood."

"Like you said, probably won't be anyone around. So it'll be nice and quiet."

Q snorted. "'Cause we'll be deaf ten seconds after we get down there."

"It'll be an adventure. Kind of our own little mountain climbing expedition. All that carbon monoxide'll probably even give us that brain buzz high-altitude guys are always raving about."

"Mountain climbers go *up*," Q snapped. But by this time, they were already walking.

Halfway down the block, Ferdinand quickened his pace, and Q matched him wordlessly. The Transitway, he thought, couldn't be much emptier than the street where he lived. Heat hummed in his skin. His footsteps sounded hollow, the way the Wiffle bat had when Q bounced it off the ground. And he kept catching his own shadowed, blurry reflection beneath layers of grime in the windows of parked cars. It was like seeing a home movie of himself twenty years older, crouched forward, inching his way to market at that lurching pace only the ancient and sick could bear. Except there wouldn't be any movies, because no one would take them. And who would watch?

The roar intensified. Glancing up, Ferdinand saw the entrance to the Transitway station and stopped. Q stopped beside him.

Flung upward from the sidewalk at a 45-degree angle, a giant wing of glinting steel loomed like the wedged-open lid of a tank, shading the escalator that dropped prospective passengers out of the neighborhood into the maelstrom of the 110. Several of the stations along the route bore similar architectural flourishes, apparently meant to signal the arrival of a new prosperity to even the most scarred and embarrassing sections of Los Angeles. Even if all they really marked were the exits.

Shielding their eyes against the beams of glare shooting off the steel overhang, Ferdinand and Q crossed Adams against the light, neglecting even to check the traffic, since there wasn't any. The cramping sensation crept all the way into Ferdinand's shoulders, now, and his steps got even faster. The excitement he felt was oddly nostalgic. When had he last experienced anything like it? Years and years ago. Maybe when his mother took him on the one and only plane ride of his childhood...or that time—*with Q*—going on Space Mountain at Disneyland. On some Grad Night excursion as chaperones for the students, maybe. *Had Florence-Normandie really taken students to Disneyland, once? They must have.* Striding even faster, waving behind him at his friend, he passed into the shadows beneath the overhang, reached the top of the escalator, and his mouth fell open as the sound surged up the shaft to meet him.

He'd been standing there several seconds, gaping, when he realized Q was tugging on his arm and turned.

Q was staring down the escalator at the noise. Even Ferdinand's hips were cramping, now. Standing in that spot really was like being atop the caldera of a volcano bubbling toward eruption. Under their feet, the whole planet seemed to shudder as millions of tons of metal and rubber and cargo and drivers crawled and snarled and fought their way home or away from home along the so-called freeways. Even up here, the din bored into their ears, and not only their ears. Ferdinand could feel it drilling into the corners of his eyes and the top of his skull and the cartilage of his rib cage.

And then there was the exhaust, which he half-believed he could see rippling in the air at the bottom of the escalator. It didn't exactly float, any more than smog on the horizon did. It lapped, instead. Here at last was the manmade reservoir the people of L.A. had always dreamed of building, deep and renewable enough to sustain life in this city where nothing but desert tortoises and creosote should live. As long as the new inhabitants could drink and breathe carbon monoxide instead of water.

"Let's do it," he finally said. "Be like our own private limo once the bus comes."

"Got that right," Q half-shouted. "Don't see anyone else stupid enough to join us."

Ferdinand stepped onto the escalator, which whisked him silently down. He'd gone maybe fifty feet when the surging sound finally swept up and engulfed him. Jamming his palms against his ears, he half-turned, saw Q still poised at the top, not yet descending, and almost panicked. He didn't want to be down here alone, and somewhere in the onslaught of traffic noise the tunnel caught and magnified there were other sounds. *From inside his head?* A small child's laughter, and whistling—*like a Wiffle curving as it caught the air?*—and something else, too. Ferdinand lifted his right-hand palm a tiny bit away from his ear, just to check. Then he dropped his hands altogether.

That last sound, anyway, had come from the walls. *A voice?* Not exactly. *An articulated breath*? A consonant in the burbling, snarling torrent.

Dddd.

Hands at his sides, whole head ringing, Ferdinand glided down, watching Q recede out of sight. He could taste carbon monoxide slithering between his clenched teeth and down his windpipe. Just as he reached the bottom, he began to bounce up and down on his heels and opened his mouth, wanting to warn Q, shriek for him to go back. Then he just stood still, listening.

What he heard was roaring from the freeway, full of overtones, vibrating all the way down his bones. No laughter. No whistling. He was standing in a cylindrical concrete walkway, brightly lit. He couldn't see any tagging anywhere, just bright, cheerful colors winking off the walls and ceiling. So the city had continued pouring funds into keeping these places bright and clean and usable, even if they were deafening. Or else even the gangs wouldn't come down here.

The walls and ceiling were actually chrome, Ferdinand realized. The colors came from reflected sunlight shooting off the hoods and roofs of the thousand cars and trucks passing every minute out there, twenty feet ahead, where the tunnel opened onto broad daylight and the shelterless island of the Transitway station.

"My friend, the Sun—like all my friends
Inconstant, lovely, far away..."

Those were the words his father had used to propel himself north, through a silence all but unimaginable, now, to a promised land that had, in some ways, kept its promises. His father had never landed a job worthy of his education. But Ferdinand had. And now he stood here, using the same words just to propel himself onto a bus so he could go downtown.

It was a mercy, he supposed, the way people's capacity for adventure seemed to decrease along with their opportunities for it.

"At least drowning's supposedly *quiet*," Q shouted as he stepped off the escalator and stood next to Ferdinand.

"What?" Ferdinand shouted back.

Instead of laughing, Q ducked, and Ferdinand did too, instinctively, as that hard *Dddd* he'd heard before erupted out of the ceiling like hail. When it stopped, both men straightened, glanced up the walls, and finally at each other. Ferdinand was surprised to find his hands at chest level, curled into fists, one on top of the other, as though cocking a bat. *Milt. Julio. Milt. Playing Bond-and-Blofeld in the dark as the* cookie *flashed overhead, that's what they'd called that splotch-asteroid that appeared right as they topped Space Mountain's lone hill...*

Sticking out a hand to steady himself against the wall, Ferdinand shook himself hard, felt whatever he'd been thinking fly to pieces. His fingers seemed to sink into the concrete. When he stumbled forward a step, he seemed to pass through strands of carbon monoxide hanging in mid-air like cobwebbing.

"You hear a dog?" Q yelled.

Ferdinand turned slowly, eyeing his friend.

Q shrugged. "For a second, swore I heard Benjamins."

"Listen hard enough down here, you'll hear anything you want to," Ferdinand said, but too quietly. Even he couldn't hear himself. "Benjamins?"

"My..." Q started. Then he just stood. Slowly, as though he were liquid, a shudder rippled over his still-massive shoulders.

"Q. You don't have a —"

"Got to cut down on the pre-noon Coronas don't I? Remind me, yeah?"

Ferdinand began to nod, and the shudder caught him, too. *Because of the way Q said the dog's name. As though...*

Then he heard barking. Stiffening, Ferdinand glanced fast toward the walls, blinking away the blinding streaks of color. When his vision cleared, he was looking up at a shiny reflection of himself upside down. A paunchy wannabe-*gringo* in a button-up shirt two sizes too big, floating bewildered in a sea of pavement. Why wouldn't there be dogs here? It was as good a place as any to shit and scavenge and wrestle for dominance with your friends and get run over and die.

Q, he noticed, was not looking. He was staring straight ahead. Slowly, he put his hand out, turned it over, as though awaiting a lick. And at that moment, Ferdinand thought he felt it, too. A trace of warm wetness across his palm, heavy golden paws on his chest, but there was nothing, nothing, never had been...

Yanking his hands up from his sides where they'd been dangling, Ferdinand realized that his ears were literally quivering against his head, trying to fold like evening primroses fleeing light. He jammed his palms to his temples again. What he'd heard wasn't dogs, or *Dddd*, either. That was just the scrambled sense his brain was trying to make from the din.

Benjamins, Bond-and-Blofeld, Milt and Julio, piñatas and Robin Hood bowls, Petra laughing...

Spinning so fast he almost twisted right off his feet, Ferdinand took two fast steps back the way he'd come. He was saying something, too, shouting, maybe just making sound, trying to cancel out the racket the way noise-blocking headphones supposedly did. His eyes had started to stream —*from exhaust, just exhaust, it was probably healthier to hike across Bikini Island after a nuclear test than to spend fifteen minutes down here*—and now he was singing. The Bond theme, the guitar bit, *dung-de-de-dungdung-de-duh-duh.*

There *had* been an up escalator, hadn't there? He hadn't noticed. Sweat broke out all over him, and without lowering his hands or stopping humming or opening his eyes any wider than he had to, he scurried back to the bottom of the shaft from which he'd descended, and yes, there it was, gliding silently up. The way out. Home. He took another step, and Q grabbed his shoulder from behind, turned him, and as he saw his friend's face once more, Ferdinand smiled a single, desperate smile, and said, "Petra."

Q's fingers tightened, dug hard into Ferdinand's skin. "What the fuck did you just say?"

Ignoring the pain—relishing it, really, so sharp, so undeniably *there*, the first time in so unspeakably long—Ferdinand reached up and touched Q's hand with his own. "I said my wife's name." His eyes welled and overflowed. "My wife's name was Petra."

Around them, barking erupted again, louder this time, more distinct. When Ferdinand craned his neck, he saw his overhead reflection swarmed by thousands of flashes of color, as though set upon by sharks in a frenzy. He couldn't stay here. Not in this tunnel. Not one more second. And the fastest way out wasn't up, but straight. Onto the freeway. Ripping free of Q's hand, barely registering his friend's gaping, terrified face, Ferdinand flung himself forward.

Seconds later, he was doubled over gagging in the sunlight. Eventually, he felt blindly with his hand, found the mesh metal bench the city had thoughtfully provided to mark the bus stop, and sat down. For a long time, he concentrated on trying to breathe. Behind him, the sounds continued to swirl, rioting in their cavern. *Petra.* Nothing else. Just the name. And the certainty. Ferdinand felt tears mass in his eyes again, let them come, held on tight to the bench as the passing traffic rattled him.

Finally, Q emerged, too, stumbled to the bench, sat down. Another long minute passed before Ferdinand realized he was sobbing.

"Milt," Q said, through the fingers curtaining his face. "My son."

Which was right. Of course it was. For Christ's sake, when Julio had been very young there was no one on earth, not even Ferdinand and Petra, that Julio had wanted to see more than—

Julio.

DDDD, wailed the voices behind him. *Dddddaaaahhh.*

Half-screaming now, as the wind of two massive trucks thundered over him, he looked down, one last time, at his hands.

Fist on top of fist. Batting position. Ferdinand surged fully awake in one headlong, convulsive rush.

The cookie on the ceiling of Space Mountain. The furniture in the guest room, which had never been a guest room. Bunk bed, plastered with L.A. Raiders stickers. Poster of Farrah in that hideous brown bathing suit upside down right next to the head of the top bunk, "So she's always looking right at me, and only at me, Pops." Bukowski on the bookshelves, which Ferdinand had railed against, hoping his disapproval would disguise at least some of his pride at his boy's discovery of such writing at the age of twelve.

His son's room. His *son's room*. Even through his own screams, he could hear Q's, took half a moment to wonder what *he'd* just remembered. Then Ferdinand was saying Julio's name again. Just the name, turning it in his mouth like a key in a lock, feeling it click, watching his whole life swing open.

Milt and Julio together. Striking each other out with the Wiffle, demanding constantly to be left alone, to go off alone, go downtown, take the bus...

"Oh, no," he said, and somehow, through the aching that gripped his entire frame like a vise, he sat up. "Oh, no."

They'd come here. Julio. Petra. Milt. All. Sooner or later. How long ago? How fucking long?

Right then, glancing to his right down the freeway, Ferdinand saw the bus. Giant, empty, shambling straight toward them. A year or two ago—it was almost funny, not funny at all, that he could remember this but not his family—Q had showed up outside Ferdinand's classroom door outraged, waving a newspaper. He'd waltzed right into Ferdinand's first-period class and brandished the paper at the students. *"You don't exist,"* he'd practically shouted. *"It's right here in the paper. You don't exist."* The article he'd been waving had come from the Sunday *Times*, reporting on a City Council vote to remove the name South Central from all future maps of Los Angeles. Too many negative associations. And it hadn't ever been a *real* place, anyway. Had it? Not one you could fix a precise location to.

"One by one," Q croaked. He was all the way standing, now, staring at the bus, which crawled closer, towering over the traffic before it. Shepherding it.

"One by one," Ferdinand murmured back.

Everyone they'd cared about. Everyone they'd loved. Everyone around them. One by one, each for their own reasons, they'd glided down those escalators and stepped aboard the Transitway, which had swallowed not only them but the memory of them, wiping them clean out of history. Was this whole thing some unthinkable top-secret city project, a logical extension of that Council vote? The runoff channel the city had needed for so many decades, to help it funnel the unnecessary and unseemly into the sea of oblivion?

Or maybe the desert had arisen at last from the distressed sand, reclaiming itself from the teeming creatures it couldn't possibly sustain.

Or was the Transitway a Transitway, after all, a service that simply shuttled riders elsewhere?

"Come on," Q said, grabbing Ferdinand's elbow and trying to tug him back toward the tunnel.

Ferdinand just opened his mouth, turned, and stared. "Come on? Where?"

"Anywhere. It's coming, you idiot. *Run!*"

"Run *where?*" Both of them were shouting. It was the only way to be heard. Behind them, the sounds in the tunnel seemed to have cohered into a rumbling, feline snarl. "Q, I'm going where the bus goes."

"It goes *nowhere*, man. Don't you get it?"

"It goes where they went. Where else would you want to be?"

"Right fucking here, dude. Where I can remember. Where I can grieve. You go cop out. I'm taking their lives back with me. Or their memories, anyway. I persevere, and I *preserve*. It's what I've been doing my whole life."

In the tunnel, the snarling intensified. When Ferdinand looked toward it, the light in there seemed to have dimmed. "Q," he said. "I'm not sure we actually have a choice."

"One way to find out."

Without another word or a good-bye glance, Q launched himself off the traffic island and ran straight for the tunnel. Ferdinand almost went after him, though whether to drag him back or follow he couldn't have said, then caught sight of the bus inching closer. All but here. He stopped, stared at it a second, looked back toward Q.

It was like watching a car back over one of those rows of angled spikes set up next to signs reading DO NOT BACK UP—SEVERE TIRE DAMAGE. At the mouth of the tunnel, Q took a little leap, and so he wasn't even touching the ground when his body shredded. It simply came apart in the air, in dozens of pieces, and Ferdinand fell to his knees screaming and weeping, but he couldn't close his eyes.

The most astonishing part, in the end, was the absence of blood. Each shining sliver of Q seemed to shoot straight up, like a spark ejected from a fire, and for that one moment, all the things he was and knew seemed to hover in the air, all jumbled up, a kaleidoscope of bone and books and beer and muscle and love of kids and quiet, seething desperation. And then it vanished. Every speck.

Falling forward onto his hands, Ferdinand crouched, rocking, blowing heaving breaths through his lips. Tasting the fouled, poisoned air. Remembering.

Then, slowly, he stood, turned. The bus had come, was sliding into the station with a weirdly human breath that seemed to echo all the way across the endless lanes of endless traffic.

Black hair. His wife had had black hair. She'd worn a clip in it, every single day, right at the base of her neck. Clenching his jaw, Ferdinand tried to remember more. But nothing came. Not now. Not yet. *Soon.* He'd see them soon. Petra. Julio.

Or else he wouldn't. Regardless, he was going. Either way, he wouldn't be alone anymore. He hadn't ever been, not in the way he'd imagined all these…however many years it had been.

Years, though. He allowed himself one quiet prayer: that the Transitway had taken Q, too. That all ways out of this place led somewhere, or at least to the same nowhere. Drying his eyes on the drooping sleeves of his ridiculous blue shirt, Ferdinand stepped toward the bus as the doors sighed open.

The Muldoon

"He found that he could not even concentrate for more than an
instant on Skeffington's death, for Skeffington, alive,
in multiple guises, kept getting in the way."
—Edwin O'Connor

That night, like every night we spent in our grandfather's house,
my older brother Martin and I stayed up late to listen.
Sometimes, we heard murmuring in the white, circular vent high
up the cracking plaster wall over our heads. The voices were our
parents', we assumed, their conversation captured but also
muffled by the pipes in the downstairs guest room ceiling. In
summer, when the wind went still between thunderstorms, we
could almost make out words. Sometimes, especially in August,
when the Baltimore heat strangled even the thunderclouds, we
heard cicadas bowing wildly in the grass out our window and
twenty feet down.

On the dead-still September night after my grandfather's
shiva, though, when all of the more than two thousand well-
wishers we'd hosted that week had finally filed through the
house and told their stories and left, all Martin and I heard was
the clock. *Tuk, tuk, tuk*, like a prison guard's footsteps. I could
almost see it out there, hulking over the foyer below, nine feet of
carved oak and that bizarre, glassed-in face, brass hands on
black velvet with brass fittings. Even though the carvings all the
way up the casing were just wiggles and flourishes, and even
though the velvet never resembled anything but a blank, square
space, the whole thing had always reminded me more of a totem
pole than a clock, and it scared me, some.

"Miriam," my brother whispered. "Awake?"

I hesitated until after the next *tuk*. It had always seemed bad luck to start a sentence in rhythm with that clock. "Think they're asleep?"

He sat up. Instinctively, my glance slipped out our open door to the far hallway wall. My grandfather had died right out there, felled at last by the heart attack his physician had warned him for decades was coming if he refused to drop fifty pounds. It seemed impossible that his enormous body had left not the slightest trace in the threadbare hallway carpet. What had he even been doing up here? In the past four years or so, I'd never once seen him more than two steps off the ground floor.

The only thing I could see in the hallway now was the mirror. Like every other mirror in the house, it had been soaped for the *shiva*, and so, instead of the half-reassuring, half-terrifying blur of movement I usually glimpsed there, I saw only darkness, barely penetrated by the single butterfly nightlight plugged in beneath it.

Reaching over the edge of the bed, I found my sweatpants and pulled them on under my nightgown. Then I sat up, too.

"Why do they soap the mirrors?"

"Because the Angel of Death might still be lurking. You don't want him catching sight of you." Martin turned his head my way, and a tiny ray of light glinted off his thick owl-glasses.

"That isn't why," I whispered.

"You make the ball?"

"Duh."

With a quick smile that trapped moonlight in his braces, my brother slid out of bed. I flipped my own covers back but waited until he reached the door, poked his head out, and peered downstairs. Overhead, the vent pushed a useless puff of cold air into the heat that had pooled around us. In the foyer, the clock *tuk*-ed.

"*Voices*," I hissed, and Martin scampered fast back to bed. His glasses tilted toward the vent. I grinned. "Ha. We're even."

Now I could see his eyes, dark brown with huge irises, as

though bulging with all the amazing things he knew. One day, thought, if Martin kept reading like he did, badgered my parents into taking him to enough museums, just stood there and *watched* the way he could sometimes, he'd literally pop himself like an over-inflated balloon.

"For what?" he snapped.

"That Angel of Death thing."

"That's what Roz told me."

"She would."

He grinned back. "You're right."

From under my pillow, I drew out the sock-ball I'd made and flipped it to him. He turned it in his hands as though completing an inspection. Part of the ritual. Once or twice, he'd even torn balls apart and made me redo them. The dayglow-yellow stripes my mother hoped looked just a little athletic on his spindle-legs had to curve just so, like stitching on a baseball. And the weight had to be right. Three, maybe four socks, depending on how worn they were and what brand mom had bought. Five, and the thing just wouldn't arc properly.

"You really think we should play tonight?"

Martin glanced up, as though he hadn't even considered that. Then he shrugged. "Grandpa would've."

I knew that he'd considered it plenty. And that gave me my first conscious inkling of just how much our grandfather had meant to my brother.

This time, I followed right behind Martin to the door, and we edged together onto the balcony. Below us, hooded in shadow, stood the grandfather clock and the double-doored glass case where Roz, the tall, orange-skinned, sour-faced woman Grandpa had married right after I was born, kept her porcelain poodles and her milky blue oriental vases. Neither Martin nor I thought of Roz as our grandma, exactly, though she was the only one we'd known, and our mother had ordered us to call her that. Beyond the foyer, I could just see the straightened rows of chairs we'd set up for the week's last mourner's *kaddish*, the final chanting of words that seemed to have channeled a permanent groove on my tongue. The older you get, my mother had told me, the more familiar they become. *Yit-barah, v'yish-tabah, v'yit-pa-ar, v'yit-roman, v'yit-na-sey...*

"You can throw first," my brother said, as though granting me a favor.

"Don't you want to?" I teased. "To honor him?" Very quietly, I began to make chicken clucks.

"Cut it out," Martin mumbled, but made no move toward the stairs. I clucked some more, and he shot out his hand so fast I thought he was trying to hit me. But he was only flapping in that nervous, spastic wave my parents had been waiting for him to outgrow since he was three. "*Shush.* Look."

"I am look..." I started, then realized he wasn't peering over the balcony at the downstairs hall from which Roz would emerge to scream at us if she heard movement. He was looking over his shoulder toward the mirror. "Not funny," I said.

"Weird," said Martin. Not until he took a step across the landing did I realize what he meant.

The doors to the hags' rooms were open. Not much. I couldn't see anything of either room. But both had been pushed just slightly back from their usual positions. Clamminess flowed from my fingertips up the peach fuzz on my arms.

Naturally, halfway across the landing, Martin stopped. If I didn't take the lead, he'd never move another step. The clammy sensation spread to my shoulders, down my back. I went to my brother anyway. We stood, right in the spot where the mirror should have reflected us. Right where Grandpa died. In the butterfly-light, Martin's face looked wet and waxy, the way it did when he had a fever.

"You really want to go through those doors?" I whispered.

"Just trying to remember."

I nodded first toward Mrs. Gold's room, then Sophie's. "Pink. Blue." The shiver I'd been fighting for the past half-minute snaked across my ribs.

Martin shook his head. "I mean the last time we saw them open. Either one."

But he already knew that. So did I. We'd last glimpsed those rooms the week before the hags had died. Four years—almost half my life—ago.

"Let's not," I said, and Martin shuffled to the right, toward Mrs. Gold's. "Martin, come on, let's play. I'm going downstairs."

But I stayed put, amazed, as he scuttled forward with his eyes darting everywhere, like a little ghost-shrimp racing across an exposed patch of sea bottom. *He'll never do it*, I thought, *not without me*. I tried chicken-clucking again, but my tongue had dried out. Martin stretched out his hand and shoved.

The door made no sound as it glided back, revealing more shadows, the dark humps of four-poster bed and dresser, a square of moonlight through almost-drawn curtains. A split second before, if someone had asked me to sketch Mrs. Gold's room, I would have made a big, pink smear with a crayon. But now, even from across the hall, I recognized that everything was just the way I'd last seen it.

"Coming?" Martin asked.

More than anything else, it was the plea in his voice that pulled me forward. I didn't bother stopping, because I knew I'd be the one going in first anyway. But I did glance at my brother's face as I passed. His skin looked even waxier than before, as though it might melt right off.

Stopping on the threshold, I reached into Mrs. Gold's room with my arm, then jerked it back.

"*What?*" my brother snapped.

I stared at the goose bumps dimpling the skin above my wrist like bubbles in boiling water. But the air in Mrs. Gold's room wasn't boiling. It was freezing cold. "I think we found this house's only unclogged vent," I said.

"Just flick on the lights."

I reached in again. It really was freezing. My hand danced along the wall. I was imagining fat, pink spiders lurking right above my fingers, waiting while I stretched just that last bit closer...

"Oh, *fudder*," I mumbled, stepped straight into the room, and switched on the dresser lamp. The furniture leapt from its shadows into familiar formation, *surprise!* But there was nothing surprising. How was it that I remembered this so perfectly, having spent a maximum of twenty hours in here in my entire life, none of them after the age of six?

There it all was, where it had always been: the bed with its crinoline curtain and beige sheets that always looked too heavy and scratchy to me, something to make drapes out of, not sleep in; the pink wallpaper; the row of perfect pink powder puffs laid atop closed pink clam-lids full of powder or God-knows-what, next to dark pink bottles of lotion; the silver picture frame with the side-by-side posed portraits of two men in old army uniforms. Brothers? Husbands? Sons? I'd been too young to ask. Mrs. Gold was Roz's mother, but neither of them had ever explained about the photographs, at least not in my hearing. I'm not sure even my mother knew.

As Martin came in behind me, the circular vent over the bed gushed frigid air. I clutched my arms tight against myself and closed my eyes and was surprised to find tears between my lashes. Just a few. Every visit to Baltimore for the first six years of my life, for one hour per day, my parents would drag chairs in here and plop us down by this bed to *chat* with Mrs. Gold. That was my mother's word for it. Mostly, what we did was sit in the chairs or — when I was a baby — crawl over the carpet and make silent faces at each other while Mrs. Gold prattled endlessly, senselessly, about horses or people we didn't know with names like Ruby and Selma, gobbling the Berger cookies we brought her and scattering crumbs all over those scratchy sheets. My mother would nod and smile and wipe the crumbs away. Mrs. Gold would nod and smile, and strands of her poofy white hair would blow in the wind from the vent. As far as I could tell, Mrs. Gold had no idea who any of us were. All those hours in here, and really, we'd never even met her.

Martin had slipped past me, and now he touched the fold of the sheet at the head of the bed. I was amazed again. He'd done the same thing at the funeral home, stunning my mother by sticking his hand into the coffin during the visitation and gently, with one extended finger, touching my grandfather's lapel. Not typical timid Martin behavior.

"Remember her hands?" he said.

Like shed snakeskin. So dry no lotion on earth, no matter how pink, would soften them

"She seemed nice," I said, feeling sad again. For Grandpa, mostly, not Mrs. Gold. After all, we'd never known her when she was...whoever she was. "I bet she was nice."

Martin took his finger off the bed and glanced at me. "Unlike the one we were actually related to." And he walked straight past me into the hall.

"Martin, no." I paused only to switch out the dresser lamp. As I did, the clock in the foyer *tuk*-ed, and the dark seemed to pounce on the bed, the powder puffs, and the pathetic picture frame. I hurried into the hall, conscious of my clumping steps. Was I *trying* to wake Roz?

Martin stood before Sophie's door, hand out, but he hadn't touched it. When he turned to me, he had a grin on his face I'd never seen before. *"Momzer,"* he drawled.

My mouth dropped open. He sounded exactly like her. "Stop it."

"Come to Gehenna. Suffer with me."

"Martin, *shut up!*"

He flinched, bumped Sophie's door with his shoulder and then stumbled back in my direction. The door swung open, and we both held still and stared.

Balding carpet, yellow-white where the butterfly light barely touched it. Everything else stayed shadowed. The curtains in there had been drawn completely. When was the last time light had touched this room?

"Why did you say that?" I asked

"It's what she said. To Grandpa, every time he dragged himself up here. Remember?"

"What's *momzer?*"

Martin shook his head. "Aunt Paulina slapped me once for saying it."

"What's *henna?*"

"*Gehenna.* One sixtieth of Eden."

Prying my eyes from Sophie's doorway, I glared at my brother. "What does that mean?"

"It's like Hell. Jew Hell."

"Jews don't believe in Hell. Do we?"

"Somewhere wicked people go. They can get out, though. After they suffer enough."

"Can we play our game now?" I made a flipping motion with my hand, cupping it as though around a sock-ball.

"Let's...take one look. Pay our respects."

"Why?"

Martin looked at the floor, and his arms gave one of their half-flaps. "Grandpa did. Every day she was alive, no matter what she called him. If we don't, no one ever will again."

He strode forward, pushed the door all the way back, and actually stepped partway over the threshold. The shadows leaned toward him, and I made myself move, thinking I might need to catch him if he fainted. With a flick of his wrist, Martin switched on the lights.

For a second, I thought the bulbs had blown, because the shadows glowed rather than dissipated, and the plain, boxy bed in there seemed to take slow shape, as though reassembling itself. Then I remembered. Sophie's room wasn't blue because of wallpaper or bed coverings or curtain fabric. She'd liked dark blue light, barely enough to see by, just enough to read if you were right under the lamp. She'd lain in that light all day, curled beneath her covers with just her thin, knife-shaped head sticking out like a moray eel's.

Martin's hand had found mine, and after a few seconds, his touch distracted me enough to glance away, momentarily, from the bed, the bare dresser, the otherwise utterly empty room. I stared down at our palms. *"Your brother's only going to love a few people,"* my mother had told me once, after he'd slammed the door to his room in my face for the thousandth time so he could do experiments with his chemistry set or read Ovid aloud to himself without me bothering him. *"You'll be one of them."*

"How'd they die?" I asked.

Martin seemed transfixed by the room, or his memories of it, which had to be more defined than mine. Our parents had never made us come in here. But Martin had accompanied Grandpa, at least some of the time. When Sophie wasn't screaming, or calling everyone names. He took a long time answering. "They were old."

"Yeah. But didn't they, like, die on the same day or something?"

"Same week, I think. Dad says that happens a lot to old people. They're barely still in their bodies, you know? Then someone they love goes, and it's like unbuckling the last straps holding them in. They just slip out."

"But Sophie and Mrs. Gold hated each other."

Martin shook his head. "Mrs. Gold didn't even know who Sophie was, I bet. And Sophie hated everything. You know, Mom says she was a really good person until she got sick. Super smart, too. She used to give lectures at the synagogue."

"Lectures about what?"

"Hey," said Martin, let go of my hand, and took two shuffling steps into Sophie's room. Blue light washed across his shoulders, darkening him. On the far wall, something twitched. Then it rose off the plaster. I gasped, lunged forward to grab Martin, and a second something joined the first, and I understood.

"No one's been in here," I whispered. The air was not cold, although the circular vent I could just make out over the bed coughed right as I said that. Another thought wriggled behind my eyes, but I shook it away. "Martin, the mirror."

Glancing up, he saw what I meant. The glass on Sophie's wall—the wall facing the hall, not the bed, she'd never wanted to see herself—stood unsoaped, pulling the dimness in rather than reflecting it, like a black hole. In that light, we were just shapes, our faces featureless. Even for Grandpa's *shiva*, no one had bothered to prepare this room.

Martin turned from our reflections to me, his pointy nose and glasses familiar and reassuring, but only until he spoke.

"Miriam, look at this."

Along the left-hand wall ran a long closet with sliding wooden doors. The farthest door had been pulled almost all the way open and tipped off its runners, so that it hung half-sideways like a dangling tooth.

"Remember the dresses?"

I had no idea what he was talking about now. I also couldn't resist another glance in the mirror, but then quickly pulled my eyes away. There were no pictures on Sophie's bureau, just a heavy, wooden gavel. My grandfather's, of course. He must have given it to her when he retired.

"This whole closet used to be stuffed with them. Fifty, sixty, maybe more, in plastic cleaner's bags. I don't think she ever wore them after she moved here. I can't even remember her getting dressed."

"She never left the room," I muttered.

"Except to sneak into Mrs. Gold's."

I closed my eyes as the clock *tuk*-ed and the vent rasped.

It had only happened once while we were in the house. But Grandpa said she did it all the time. Whenever Sophie got bored of accusing her son of kidnapping her from her own house and penning her up here, or whenever her ravaged, rotting lungs allowed her enough breath, she'd rouse herself from this bed, inch out the door in her bare feet with the blue veins popping out of the tops like rooster crests, and sneak into Mrs. Gold's room. There she'd sit, murmuring God knew what, until Mrs. Gold started screaming.

"It always creeped me out," Martin said. "I never liked looking over at this closet. But the dresses blocked *that*."

"Blocked wh—" I started, and my breath caught in my teeth. Waist-high on the back inside closet wall, all but covered by a rough square of wood that had been leaned against it rather than fitted over it, there was an opening. A door. "Martin, if Roz catches us in here—"

Hostility flared in his voice like a lick of flame. "Roz hardly ever catches us playing the balcony ball game right outside her room. Anyway, in case you haven't noticed, she *never* comes in here."

"What's with you?" I snapped. Nothing about my brother made sense tonight.

"What? Nothing. It's just...Grandpa brings Roz's mother here, even though she needs constant care, can't even feed herself unless she's eating Berger cookies, probably has no idea where she is. Grandpa takes care of her, like he took care of everyone. But when it comes to *his* mother, Roz won't even bring food in here. She makes him do everything. And after they die, Roz leaves her own mother's room exactly like it was, but she cleans out every trace of Sophie, right down to the closet."

"Sophie was mean."

"She was sick. And ninety-two."

"And mean."

"I'm going in there," Martin said, gesturing or flapping, I couldn't tell which. "I want to see Grandpa's stuff. Don't you? I bet it's all stored in there."

"I'm going to bed. Good night, Martin."

In an instant, the hostility left him, and his expression turned small, almost panicked.

"I'm going to bed," I said again.

"You don't want to see Grandpa?"

This time, the violence in my own voice surprised me. "Not in there." I was thinking of the way he'd looked in his coffin. His dead face had barely even resembled his real one. His living one. His whole head had been transformed by the embalming into a shiny, vaguely Grandpa-shaped *bulge* balanced atop his bulgy, overweight body, like the top of a snowman.

"Please," Martin said, and something moved downstairs.

"Shit," I mouthed, going completely still.

Clock tick. Clock tick. Footsteps. *Had I left the lights on in Mrs. Gold's room?* I couldn't remember. If Roz wasn't looking, she might not see Sophie's blue light from downstairs. Somehow, I knew she didn't want us in here.

I couldn't help glancing behind me, and then my shoulders clenched. The door had swung almost all the way shut.

Which wasn't so strange, was it? How far had we even opened it?

Footsteps. Clock tick. Clock tick. Clock tick. Clock tick. When I turned back to Martin, he was on his hands and knees, scuttling for the closet.

"Martin, *no*," I hissed. Then I was on my knees too, hurrying after him. When I drew up alongside him, our heads just inside the closet, he looked my way and grinned, tentatively.

"Sssh," he whispered.

"What do you think you'll find in there?"

The grin slid from his face. "Him." With a nod, he pulled the square of wood off the opening. Then he swore and dropped it. His right hand rose to his mouth, and I saw the sliver sticking out of the bottom of his thumb like a porcupine quill.

Taking his wrist, I leaned over, trying to see. In that murky, useless light, the wood seemed to have stabbed straight through the webbing into his palm. It almost looked like a new ridge forming along his lifeline. "Hold still," I murmured, grabbed the splinter as low down as I could, and yanked.

Martin sucked in breath, staring at his hand. "Did you get it all?"

"Come where it's light and I'll see."

"No." He pulled his hand from me, and without another word crawled through the opening. For one moment, as his butt hovered in front of me and his torso disappeared, I had to stifle another urge to drag him out, splinters be damned. Then he was through. For a few seconds, I heard only his breathing, saw only his bare feet through the hole. The rest of him was in shadow.

"Miriam, get in here," he said.

In I went. I had to shove Martin forward to get through, and I did so harder than I had to. He made no protest. I tried lifting my knees instead of sliding them, to keep the splinters off. When I straightened, I was surprised to find most of the space in front of us bathed in moonlight.

"What window is that?" I whispered.

"Must be on the side."

"I've never seen it."

"How much time have you spent on the side?"

None, in truth. No one did. The space between my grandfather's house and the ancient gray wooden fence that bordered his property had been overrun by spiders even when our mom was young. I'd glimpsed an old bike back there once, completely draped in webs like furniture in a dead man's room.

"Probably a billion spiders in here too, you know," I said.

But Martin wasn't paying attention, and neither was I, really. We were too busy staring. All around us, stacked from floor to four-foot ceiling all the way down the length of the half-finished space, cardboard boxes had been stacked, sometimes atop each other, sometimes atop old white suitcases or trunks with their key-coverings dangling like the tongues on strangled things. With his shoulder, Martin nudged one of the nearest stacks, which tipped dangerously but slid back a bit. Reaching underneath a lid flap, Martin stuck his hand in the bottom-most box. I bit my cheek and held still and marveled, for the hundredth time in the last fifteen minutes, at my brother's behavior. When he pulled out a *Playboy*, I started to laugh, and stopped because of the look on Martin's face.

He held the magazine open and flat across both hands, looking terrified to drop it, almost in awe of it, as though it were a Torah scroll. It would be a long time, I thought, before Martin started dating.

"You said you wanted to see Grandpa's stuff," I couldn't resist teasing.

"This wasn't his."

Now I did laugh. "Maybe it was Mrs. Gold's."

I slid the magazine off his hands, and that seemed to relieve him, some. The page to which it had fallen open showed a woman with waist-length brown hair and strangely pointed feet poised naked atop the gnarled roots of an oak tree, as though she'd just climbed out of the branches. The woman wasn't smiling, and I didn't like the picture at all. I closed the magazine and laid it face down on the floor.

Edging forward, Martin began to reach randomly into other boxes. I did the same. Mostly, though, I watched my brother. The moonlight seemed to pour over him in layers, coating him, so that with each passing moment he grew paler. Other than Martin's scuttling as he moved down the row on his knees, I heard nothing, not even the clock. That should have been a comfort. But the silence in that not-quite-room was worse.

To distract myself, I began to run my fingers over the boxes on my right. Their cardboard skin had sticky damp patches, bulged outward in places but sank into itself in others. From one box, I drew an unpleasantly damp, battered, black rectangular case I thought might be for pens, but when I opened it, I found four pearls strung on a broken chain, pressed deep into their own impressions in the velvet lining like little eyes in sockets. My real grandmother's, I realized. Roz liked showier jewelry.

I'd never met my mother's mother. She'd died three months before Martin was born. Dad had liked her a lot. I was still gazing at the pearls when the first gush of icy air poured over me.

Martin grunted, and I caught his wrist. We crouched and waited for the torrent to sigh itself out. Eventually, it did. Martin started to speak, and I tightened my grasp and shut him up.

Just at the end, as the gush had died…

"Martin," I whispered.

"It's the air-conditioning, Miriam. See?"

"Martin, did you hear it?"

"Duh. Look at—"

"Martin. The vents."

He wasn't listening, didn't understand. Dazed, I let him

disengage, watched him crab-walk to the next stack of boxes and begin digging. I almost started screaming at him. If I did, I now knew, the sound would pour out of the walls above our bed, and from the circular space above Mrs. Gold's window, and from Sophie's closet. Because these vents didn't connect to the downstairs guest room where our parents were, like we'd always thought. They connected the upstairs rooms and this room. And so the murmuring we'd always heard—that we'd heard as recently as twenty minutes ago—hadn't come from our parents at all. It had come from right—

"Jackpot," Martin muttered.

Ahead, wedged between the last boxes and the wall, something stirred. Flapped. Plastic. Maybe.

"Martin…"

"Hi, Grandpa."

I spun so fast I almost knocked Martin over, banging my arms instead on the plaque he was wiping free of mold and dust with the sleeve of his pajamas. Frozen air roared over us again. Up ahead, whatever it was flapped some more.

"Watch *out*," Martin snapped. He wasn't worried about me, of course. He didn't want anything happening to the plaque.

"We have to get out of here," I said.

Wordlessly, he held up his treasure. Black granite, with words engraved in it, clearly legible despite the fuzzy smear of grime across the surface. *To the Big Judge, who takes care of his own. A muldoon, and no mistake. From his friends, the Knights of Labor.*

"The Knights of Labor?"

"He knew everyone," Martin said. "They all loved him. The whole city."

This was who my grandfather was to my brother, I realized. Someone as smart and weird and defiant and solitary as he was, except that our grandfather had somehow figured out people enough to wind up a judge, a civil rights activist, a bloated and beloved public figure. Slowly, like a snake stirring, another shudder slipped down my back.

"What's a muldoon?"

"Says right here, stupid." Martin nodded at the plaque. "He took care of his own."

"We should go, Martin. Now."

"What are you talking about?"

As the house unleashed another frigid breath, he tucked the plaque lovingly against his chest and moved deeper into the attic. The plastic at the end of the row was rippling now, flattening itself. It reminded me of an octopus I'd seen in the Baltimore Aquarium once, completely changing shape to slip between two rocks.

"There," I barked suddenly, as the air expired. "Hear it?"

But Martin was busy wedging open box lids, prying out cufflinks in little boxes, a ceremonial silver shovel marking some sort of groundbreaking, a photograph of Grandpa with Earl Weaver and two grinning grounds-crew guys in the Orioles dugout. The last thing he pulled out before I moved was a book. Old, blue binding, stiff and jacketless. Martin flipped through it once, mumbled, "Hebrew," and dumped it behind him. Embossed on the cover, staring straight up at the ceiling over my brother's head, I saw a single, lidless eye.

Martin kept going, almost to the end now. The plastic had gone still, the air-conditioning and the murmurs that rode it temporarily silent. I almost left him there. If I'd been sure he'd follow — as, on almost any other occasion, he would have — that's exactly what I would have done. Instead, I edged forward myself, my hand stretching for the book. As much to get that eye hidden again as from any curiosity, I picked the thing up and opened it. Something in the binding snapped, and a single page slipped free and fluttered away like a dried butterfly I'd let loose.

"*Ayin Harah*," I read slowly, sounding out the Hebrew letters on the title page. But it wasn't the words that set me shuddering again, if only because I wasn't positive what they implied; I knew they meant "Evil Eye." But our aunt Paulina had told us that was a protective thing, mostly. Instead, my gaze locked on my great-grandmother's signature, lurking like a blue spider in the top left-hand corner of the inside cover. Then my head lifted, and I was staring at the box from which the book had come.

Not my grandfather's stuff in there. Not my grandmother's, or Roz's, either. That box—and maybe that one alone—was *hers*.

Sophie's.

I have no explanation for what happened next. I knew better. That is, I knew, already. Thought I did. I didn't want to be in the attic even one second longer, and I was scared, not curious. I crept forward and stuck my hand between the flaps anyway.

For a moment, I thought the box was empty. My hand kept sliding deeper, all the way to my elbow before I touched cloth and closed my fist over it. Beneath whatever I'd grabbed was plastic, wrapped around some kind of heavy fabric. The plastic rustled and stuck slightly to my hand like an anemone's tentacles, though everything in that box was completely dry. I pulled, and the boxes balanced atop the one I'd reached into tipped back and bumped against the wall of the attic, and my hands came out, holding the thing I'd grasped, which fell open as it touched the air.

"Grandpa with two presidents, look," Martin said from down the row, waving a picture frame without lifting his head from whatever box he was looting.

Cradled in my palms lay what could have been a *matzoh* covering, maybe for holding the *afikomen* at a seder. When I spread out the folds, though, I found dark, rust-colored circular stains in the white fabric. Again I thought of the seder, the ritual of dipping a finger in wine and then touching it to a plate or napkin as everyone chanted plagues God had inflicted upon the Egyptians. In modern Haggadahs, the ritual is explained as a symbol of Jewish regret that the Egyptian people had to bear the brunt of their ruler's refusal to free the slaves. But none of the actual ceremonial instructions say that. They just order us to chant the words. *Dam. Tzfar de'ah. Kinim. Arbeh.*

Inside the fold where *matzoh* might have been tucked, I found only a gritty, black residue. It could have been dust from the attic, or split spider sacs, or tiny dead things. But it smelled, faintly, on my fingers. An old and rotten smell, with just a hint of something else. Something worse.

Or maybe not worse. *Familiar*. I had no idea what it was. But Sophie had smelled like this.

"Martin, please," I heard myself say. But he wasn't listening. Instead, he was leaning almost *into* the last box in the row. The plastic jammed against the wall had gone utterly still. At any moment, I expected it to hump up like a wave and crash down on my brother's back. I didn't even realize my hands had slipped back inside Sophie's box until I touched wrapping again.

Gasping, I dragged my hands away, but my fingers had curled, and the plastic and the heavy fabric it swaddled came up clutched between them.

A dress, I thought, panicking, shoving backward. *From her closet.* I stared at the lump of faded material, draped half out of the box now, the plastic covering rising slightly in the stirring air.

Except it wasn't a dress. It was two dresses, plainly visible through the plastic. One was gauzy and pink, barely there, with wispy flowers stitched up the sleeves. The other, dull white and heavy, had folded itself inside the pink one, the long sleeves encircling the waist. Long, black smears spread across the back of the white dress like finger-marks. *Like fingers dipped in Sophie's residue...*

I don't think I had any idea, at first, that I'd started shouting. I was too busy scuttling backwards on my hands, banging against boxes on either side as I scrambled for the opening behind us. The air-conditioning triggered, blasting me with its breath, which didn't stink, just froze the hairs to the skin of my arms and legs. Martin had leapt to his feet, banging his head against the attic ceiling, and now he was waving his hands, trying to quiet me. But the sight of him panicked me more. The dresses on the ground between us shivered, almost rolled over, and the plastic behind him rippled madly, popping and straining against the weight that held it, all but free. My hand touched down on the *Playboy*. I imagined the tree-woman climbing out of the magazine on her pointy feet, and finally fell hard, half out of the attic opening, screaming now, banging my spine on the wood and bruising it badly.

Then there were hands on my shoulder, hard and horny and orange-ish, yanking me out of the hole and dragging me across the floor. Yellow eyes flashing fury, Roz leaned past me and ducked her head through the hole, screeching at Martin to get out. Then she stalked away, snarling *"Out"* and *"Come on."*

Never had I known her to be this angry. I'd also never been happier to see her pinched, glaring, unhappy face, the color of an overripe orange thanks to the liquid tan she poured all over herself before her daily mah-jongg games at the club where she sometimes took us swimming. Flipping over and standing, I hurried after her, the rattle of the ridiculous twin rows of bracelets that ran halfway up her arms sweet and welcome in my ears as the tolling of a dinner bell. I waited at the lip of the closet until Martin's head appeared, then fled Sophie's room.

A few seconds later, my brother emerged, the *Knights of Labor* plaque clutched against his chest, glaring bloody murder at me. But Roz took him by the shoulders, guided him back to his bed in my mother's old room, and sat him down. I followed, and fell onto my own bed. For a minute, maybe more, she stood above us and glowed even more than usual, as though she might burst into flame. Then, for the first time in all my experience of her, she crossed her legs and sat down between our beds on the filthy floor.

"Oh, kids," she sighed. "What were you doing in there?"

"Where are Mom and Dad?" Martin demanded. The shrillness in his tone made me cringe even farther back against the white wall behind me. Pushing with my feet, I dug myself under the covers and lay my head on my pillow.

"Out," Roz said, in the same weary voice. "They're on a walk. They've been cooped up here, same as the rest of us, for an entire week."

"Cooped up?" Martin's voice rose still more, and even Roz's

leathery face registered surprise. "As in, sitting *shiva?* Paying tribute to Grandpa?"

After a long pause, she nodded. "Exactly that, Martin."

From the other room, I swore I could hear the sound of plastic sliding over threadbare carpet. My eyes darted to the doorway, the lit landing, the streaks of soap in the mirror, the floor.

"How'd they die?" I blurted.

Roz's lizard eyes darted back and forth between Martin and me. "What's with you two tonight?"

"Mrs. Gold and Sophie. Please, please, please. Grandma." I didn't often call her that. She scowled even harder.

"What are you babbling about?" Martin said to me. "Roz, Miriam's been really—"

"Badly, Miriam," Roz said, and Martin went quiet. "They died badly."

Despite what she'd said, her words had a surprising, almost comforting effect on me. "Please tell me."

"Your parents wouldn't want me to."

"Please."

Settling back, Roz eyed me, then the vent overhead. I kept glancing into the hall. But I didn't hear anything now. And after a while, I only watched her. She crossed her arms over her knees, and her bracelets clanked.

"It was an accident. A horrible accident. It really was. You have to understand...you have no idea how awful those days were. May you never have such days."

"What was so awful?" Martin asked. There was still a trace of petulance in his tone. But Roz's attitude appeared to be having the same weirdly soothing effect on him as on me.

She shrugged. "In the pink room, you've got my mother. Only she's not my mother anymore. She's this sweet, stupid, chattering houseplant."

I gaped. Martin did, too, and Roz laughed, kind of, without humor or joy.

"Every single day, usually more than once, she shit all over the bed. The rest of the time, she sat there and babbled mostly nice things about cookies or owls or whatever. Places she'd never been. People she may have known, but I didn't. She never mentioned me, or my father, or my brother, or anything about our lives. It was like she'd led some completely different life, without me in it."

Roz held her knees a while. Finally, she went on. "And in the blue room, there was Sophie, who remembered everything. How it had felt to walk to the market, or lecture a roomful of professors about the *Kabbalah* or whatever other weird stuff she knew. How it had been to live completely by herself, with her books, in her own world, the way she had for twenty-two years after your great-grandfather died. Best years of her life, I think. And then, just like that, her body gave out on her. She couldn't move well. Couldn't drive. She couldn't really see. She broke her hip twice. When your grandpa brought her here, she was so angry, kids. So angry. She didn't want to die. She didn't want to be dependent. It made her mean. That's pretty much your choices, I think. Getting old—getting *that* old, anyway—makes you mean, or sick, or stupid, or lonely. Take your pick. Only you don't get to pick. And sometimes, you wind up all four."

Rustling, from the vent. The faintest hint. Or had it come from the hallway?

"Grandma, what happened?"

"An accident, Miriam. Like I said. Your goddamn grandfather…"

"You can't—" Martin started, and Roz rode him down.

"Your goddamn grandfather wouldn't put them in homes. Either one. '*Your mother's your mother.*'" When she said that, she rumbled, and sounded just like Grandpa. "'*She's no trouble. And as for my mother…it'd kill her.*'

"But having them here, kids…it was killing us. Poisoning every single day. Wrecking every relationship we had, even with each other."

Grandma looked up from her knees and straight at us. "Anyway," she said. "We had a home care service. A private nurse.

Mrs. Gertzen. She came one night a week, and a couple weekends a year when we just couldn't take it and had to get away. When we wanted to go, we called Mrs. Gertzen, left the dates, and she came and took care of both our mothers while we were gone. Well, the last time…when they died…your grandfather called her, same as always. Sophie liked Mrs. Gertzen, was probably nicer to her than anyone else. Grandpa left instructions, and we headed off to the Delaware shore for five days of peace. But Mrs. Gertzen had a heart attack that first afternoon, and never even made it to the house. And no one else on earth had any idea that my mother and Sophie were up here."

"Oh my God," I heard myself whisper, as the vent above me rasped pathetically. For the first time in what seemed hours, I became aware of the clock, *tuk*-ing away. I was imagining being trapped in this bed, hearing that sound. The metered pulse of the living world, just downstairs, plainly audible. And—for my great-grandmother and Mrs. Gold—utterly out of reach.

When I looked at Roz again, I was amazed to find tears leaking out of her eyes. She made no move to wipe them. "It must have been worse for Sophie," she half-whispered.

My mouth fell open. Martin had gone completely still as well as silent.

"I mean, I doubt my mother even knew what was happening. She probably prattled all the way to the end. If there *is* an Angel of Death, I bet she offered him a Berger cookie."

"You're…" *nicer than I thought*, I was going to say, but that wasn't quite right. *Different than I thought.*

"But Sophie. Can you imagine how horrible? How infuriating? To realize—she must have known by dinnertime—that no one was coming? She couldn't make it downstairs. We'd had to carry her to the bathroom, the last few weeks. All she'd done that past month was light candles and read her *Zohar* and mutter to herself. I'm sure she knew she'd never make it to the kitchen. I'm sure that's why she didn't try. But I think she came back to herself at the end, you know? Turned back into the person she must have been. The woman who raised your grandfather, made him who he was or at least *let* him be. Because somehow she dragged herself into my mother's room one last time. They died with their arms around each other."

The dresses, I thought. *Had they been arranged like that on purpose? Tucked together, as a memory or a monument?* Then I was shivering, sobbing, and my brother was, too. Roz sat silently between us, staring at the floor.

"I shouldn't have told you," she mumbled. "Your parents will be furious."

Seconds later, the front door opened, and our mom and dad came hurtling up the stairs, filling our doorway with their flushed, exhausted, everyday faces.

"What are you doing up?" my mother asked, moving forward fast and stretching one arm toward each of us, though we were too far apart to be gathered that way.

"I'm afraid I—" Roz started.

"Grandpa," I said, and felt Roz look at me. "We were feeling bad about Grandpa."

My mother's mouth twisted, and her eyes closed. "I know," she said. "Me, too."

I crawled over to Martin's bed. My mother held us a long time, while my father stood above her, his hands sliding from her back to our shoulders to our heads. At some point, Roz slipped silently from the room. I didn't see her go.

For half an hour, maybe more, our parents stayed. Martin showed them the plaque he'd found, and my mother seemed startled mostly by the realization of where we'd been.

"You know I forgot that room was there?" she said. "Your cousins and I used to hide in it all the time. Before the hags came."

"You shouldn't call them that," Martin said, and my mother straightened, eyes narrowed. Eventually, she nodded, and her shoulders sagged.

"You're right. And I don't think of them that way. It's just, at the end...."

"Good night, kids."

After they'd gone, switching out all the lights except the butterfly in the hall, I thought I might sleep. But every time I closed my eyes, I swore I felt something pawing at the covers, as though trying to draw them back, so that whatever it was could crawl in with me. Opening my eyes, I found the dark room, the moon outside, the spider shadows in the corners. Several times, I glanced toward my brother's bed. He was lying on his back with the plaque he'd rescued on his chest and his head turned toward the wall, so that I couldn't see whether his eyes were open. I listened to the clock ticking and the vents rasping and muttering. *A Muldoon, and no mistake*, I found myself mouthing. *Who takes care of his own.* When I tried again to close my eyes, it seemed the vent was chanting with me. *No mistake. No mistake.* My heart twisted in its socket, and its beating bounced on the rhythm of the clock's tick like a skipped stone. I think I moaned, and Martin rolled over.

"Now let's play," he said.

Immediately, I was up, grabbing the sock-ball off the table where I'd left it. I wasn't anywhere near sleep, and I wasn't scared of Roz anymore. I wanted to be moving, doing anything. And my brother still wanted me with him.

I didn't wait for Martin this time, just marched straight out to the landing, casting a single, held-breath glance at Sophie's door. Someone had pulled it almost closed again, and I wondered if the wooden covering over the opening to the attic had also been replaced. Mrs. Gold's door, I noticed, had been left open. *Pushed open?*

Squelching that thought with a shake of my head, I started down the stairs. But Martin galloped up beside me, pushed me against the wall, took the sock-ball out of my hands, and hurried ahead.

"My ups," he said.

"Your funeral," I answered, and he stopped three steps down and turned and grinned. A flicker of butterfly light danced in his glasses, which made it look as though something reflective and transparent had moved behind me. I didn't turn around, *couldn't* turn around, *turned* and found the landing empty.

"She's asleep," Martin said, and for one awful moment, I didn't know whom he meant.

Then I did, and grinned weakly back. "If you say so." Retreating upstairs, I circled around the balcony into position.

The rules of Martin-Miriam Balcony Ball were simple. The person in the foyer below tried to lob the sock-ball over the railing and have it hit the carpet anywhere on the L-shaped landing. The person on the landing tried to catch the sock and slam it to the tile down in the foyer, triggering an innings change in which both players tried to bump each other off balance as they passed on the steps, thereby gaining an advantage for the first throw of the next round. Play ended when someone had landed ten throws on the balcony, or when Roz came and roared us back to bed, or when any small porcelain animal or *tuk*-ing grandfather clock or crystal chandelier got smashed. In the five-year history of the game, that latter ending had only occurred once. The casualty had been a poodle left out atop the cabinet. This night's game lasted exactly one throw.

In retrospect, I think the hour or so between the moment our parents left and my brother's invitation to play were no more restful for Martin than they had been for me. He'd lain more still, but that had just compressed the energy the evening had given him, and now he was fizzing like a shaken pop bottle. I watched him glance toward Roz's hallway, crouch into himself as though expecting a hail of gunfire, and scurry into the center of the foyer. He looked skeletal and small, like some kind of armored beetle, and the ache that prickled up under my skin was at least partially defensive of him. He would never fill space the way our grandfather had. No one would. That ability to love people in general more than the people closest to you was a rare and only partly desirable thing. Martin, I already knew, didn't have it.

He must have been kneading the sock-ball all the way down the stairs, because as soon as he reared back and threw, one of the socks slipped free of the knot I'd made and dangled like the tail of a comet. Worse, Martin had somehow aimed straight up, so that instead of arching over the balcony, the sock-comet shot between the arms of the chandelier, knocked crystals together as it reached its apex, and then draped itself, almost casually, over the arm nearest the steps. After that, it just hung.

The chandelier swung gently left, then right. The clock *tuk*-ed like a clucking tongue.

"Shit," Martin said, and something rustled.

"*Sssh.*" I resisted yet another urge to jerk my head around. I turned slowly instead, saw Sophie's almost-closed door, Mrs. Gold's wide-open one, the butterfly light. Our room. Nothing else. If the sound I'd just heard had come from downstairs, then Roz was awake. "Get up here," I said, and Martin came, fast.

By the time he reached me, all that fizzing energy seemed to have evaporated. His shoulders had rounded, and his glasses had clouded over with his exertion. He looked at me through his own fog.

"Mir, what are we going to do?"

"What do you think we're going to do, we're going to go get it. *You're* going to go get it."

Martin wiped his glasses on his shirt, eyeing the distance between the landing where we stood and the chandelier. "We need a broom." His eyes flicked hopefully to mine. He was Martin again, all right.

I glanced downstairs to the hallway I'd have to cross to get to the broom closet. "Feel free."

"Come on, Miriam."

"You threw it."

"You're braver."

Abruptly, the naked woman from the tree in the magazine flashed in front of my eyes. I could almost see—almost *hear*—her stepping out of the photograph, balancing on those pointed feet. Tiptoeing over the splinter-riddled floor toward those wrapped-together dresses, slipping them over her shoulders.

"What?" Martin said.

"I can't."

For the second time that night, Martin took my hand. Before the last couple hours, Martin had last held my hand when I was six years old, and my mother had made him do it whenever we crossed a street, for his protection more than mine, since he was usually thinking about something random instead of paying attention.

"I have a better idea," he whispered, and pulled me toward the top of the staircase.

As soon as he laid himself flat on the top step, I knew what he was going to do. "You can't," I whispered, but what I really meant was that I didn't believe he'd dare. There he was, though, tilting onto his side, wriggling his head through the railings. His shoulders followed. Within seconds, he was resting one elbow in the dust atop the grandfather clock.

Kneeling, I watched his shirt pulse with each *tuk*, as though a second, stronger heart had taken root inside him. *Too strong,* I thought, *it could throb him to pieces.*

"Grab me," he said. "Don't let go."

Even at age ten, my fingers could touch when wrapped around the tops of his ankles. He slid out farther, and the clock came off its back legs and leaned with him. "*Fuck!*" he blurted, wiggling back as I gripped tight. The clock tipped back toward us and banged its top against the railings and rang them.

Letting go of Martin, I scrambled to my feet, ready to sprint for our beds as I awaited the tell-tale bloom of lights in Roz's hallway. Martin lay flat, breath heaving, either resigned to his fate or too freaked out to care. It seemed impossible that Roz hadn't heard what we'd just done, and anyway, she had a sort of lateral line for this kind of thing, sensing movement in her foyer the way Martin said sharks discerned twitching fish.

But this time, miraculously, no one came. Nothing moved. And after a minute or so, without even waiting for me to hold his legs, Martin slithered forward once more. I dropped down next to him, held tighter. He kept his spine straight, dropping as little of his weight as possible atop the clock. I watched his waist wedge briefly in the railings, then slip through as his arms stretched out.

It was like feeding him to something. Worse than the clock's *tuk* was the groan from its base as it started to lean again. My hands went sweaty, and my teeth clamped down on my tongue, almost startling me into letting go. I had no idea whether the tears in my eyes were fear or exhaustion or sadness for my grandfather or the first acknowledgement that I'd just heard rustling, right behind me.

"Ow," Martin said as my nails dug into his skin. But he kept sliding forward. My eyes had jammed themselves shut, so I felt rather than saw him grab the chandelier, felt it swing slightly away from him, felt his ribs hit the top of the clock and the clock start to tip.

I opened my eyes—not looking back, *not behind*, it was only the vents, had to be—and saw Roz step out of her hallway.

Incredibly, insanely, she didn't see us at first. She had her head down, bracelets jangling, hands jammed in the pockets of her shiny silver robe, and she didn't even look up until she was dead center under the chandelier, under my brother stretched full-length in mid-air twenty feet over her head with a sock in his hands. Then the clock's legs groaned under Martin's suspended weight, and the chandelier swung out, and Roz froze. For that one split second, none of us so much as breathed. And that's how I knew, even before she finally lifted her eyes. This time, I really had heard it.

"Get back," Roz said, and burst into tears.

It made no sense. I started babbling, overwhelmed by guilt I wasn't even sure was mine. "Grandma, I'm sorry. Sorry, sorry—"

"*BACK!*" she screamed. "*Get away! Get away from them.*" With startling speed, she spun and darted up the steps, still shouting.

Them. Meaning *us.* Which meant she wasn't talking to us.

The rest happened all in one motion. As I turned, my hands came off Martin's legs. Instantly, he was gone, tipping, the clock rocking forward and over. He didn't scream, maybe didn't have time, but his body flew face-first and smacked into the floor below just as Roz hurtled past and my parents emerged shouting from the guest bedroom and saw their son and the clock smashing and splintering around and atop him and I got my single glimpse of the thing on the landing.

Its feet weren't pointed, but bare and pale and swollen with veins. It wore some kind of pink, ruffled something, and its hair was white and flying. I couldn't see its face. But its movements... the arms all out of rhythm with the feet, out of order, as if they were being jerked from somewhere else on invisible strings. And the legs, the way they moved...not Mrs. Gold's mindless, surprisingly energetic glide...more of a tilting, trembling lurch. Like Sophie's.

Rooted in place, mouth open, I watched it stagger past the blacked-out mirror, headed from the pink room to the blue one.

"*Takes care of his own*," I found myself chanting, helpless to stop. "*Takes care of his own. And no mistake. No mistake.*" There had been no mistake.

Roz was waving her hands in front of her, snarling, stomping her feet as though scolding a dog. *Had she already known it was here? Or just understood, immediately?* In seconds, she and the lurching thing were in the blue room, and Sophie's door slammed shut.

"*No mistake*," I murmured, tears pouring down my face.

The door flew open again, and out Roz came. My voice wavered, sank into silence as my eyes met hers and locked. Downstairs, my father was shouting frantically into the phone for an ambulance. Roz walked, jangling, to the step above me, sat down hard, put her head on her knees and one of her hands in my hair. Then she started to weep.

Martin had fractured his spine, broken one cheekbone, his collarbone, and both legs, and he has never completely forgiven me. Sometimes I think my parents haven't, either. Certainly, they drew away from me for a long time after that, forming themselves into a sort of protective cocoon around my brother. My family traded phone calls with Roz for years. But we never went back to Baltimore, and she never came to see us.

So many times, I've lunged awake, still seeing the Sophie-Mrs. Gold creature lurching at random into my dreams. If I'd ever had the chance, I would have asked Roz only one thing: how much danger had Martin and I really been in? Would it really have hurt us? Was it inherently malevolent, a monster devouring everything it could reach? Or was it just a peculiarly Jewish sort of ghost, clinging to every last vestige of life, no matter how painful or beset by betrayal, because only in life—*this* life—is there any possibility of pleasure or fulfillment or even release?

I can't ask anyone else, because Roz is the only one other than me who knows. I have never talked about it, certainly not to Martin, who keeps the plaque he lifted from the attic that night nailed to his bedroom wall.

But I know. And sometimes, I just want to scream at all of them, make them see what's staring them right in the face, has been obvious from the moment it happened. My grandfather, the Muldoon who took care of his own, during the whole weekend he was away with Roz, never once called his mother? Never called home? Never checked in with Mrs. Gertzen, just to see how everyone was? And Mrs. Gertzen had no family? Had left no indication to the service that employed her of what jobs she might have been engaged in?

My grandfather had called Mrs. Gertzen's house before leaving for Delaware, all right. He'd learned about Mrs. Gertzen's heart attack. Then he'd weighed his shattering second marriage, his straining relationships with his children, his scant remaining healthy days, maybe even his own mother's misery.

And he'd made his decision. Taken care of his own, and no mistake. And in the end—the way they always do, whether you take care of them or not—his own had come back for him.

Story Notes
by Glen Hirshberg

American Morons: A couple summers ago, I went to a cousin's wedding in Tuscany on the weekend of the Palio. I didn't see the actual race, but I was in Siena the day afterward, and spent an entire afternoon trailing through the cobblestone streets behind the victorious Giraffa *contrada* as they drummed and sang and pranced around the city, waving and tossing flags, guiding the winning horse into the churches and courtyards of vanquished neighbors, gesturing gleefully in the faces of widows weeping on windowsills overhead. It had been several years—since the birth of my son, at least—since I'd felt myself so deliciously on the outside of a ritual, so exhilaratingly alien. The next evening, on our way back to Rome, my brother poured gasoline into a car gas tank marked with a cap reading *Diesel*, and we spent four scorching hours broken down beside the *superstrade*, before eventually receiving a tow into a neighborhood overrun with peacocks (most, but not all of them, living). My brother scrawled the titular phrase in the filthy passenger's-side window before we abandoned the car. Most of the good, self-mocking lines at the beginning of the story are his. I had the story sketched long before we made it back to Rome.

Like a Lily in a Flood: The first of two stories in this collection that originated in the discovery of a book inscription. I'd ordered a battered 1892 copy of Dante Rosetti's *Ballads and Sonnets* online because the price was right and I needed a jolt of mad poetry and the book exuded a redolence, even through my computer monitor. The redolence, alas—God, I so much prefer trolling through used books endlessly in person—proved to be smoke. But on the first inside title page, I found the following cryptic inscription:

Mary from the Counselor 1891

Jackie Chan once said in an interview that where other people walk down the streets and see buildings, he sees opportunities for mayhem. Somehow, I think part of my brain works the same way, except what I tend to see are intruding (or invented) memories. Certainly, in this case, I tumbled immediately into alarming and delicious daydreams. Later that summer, we spent a few days in a cabin on a New Hampshire lake, not far from where the historical Millerites experienced their Disappointment, and the loons let fly. I finished the first draft of *Lily* three days into our trip, propped on the dock, swatting mosquitoes while my son floated free of both my wife and me for the first time in his life....

Flowers on Their Bridles, Hooves in the Air: The place was actually called Loof's Lite-a-Line, and it was pretty much the last vestige, I think, of the now-defunct Long Beach Pike amusement park at the end of the old pier. Even today, despite a typically ruthless Southern California bout of urban renewal that has clamped metaphorical mouse ears on every street sign and crumbling shop-front, there are parts of Long Beach that still feel like themselves, which is more than I can say for most municipalities within fifty miles of it. It's also probably why this story took root there. Sadly, this Lite-a-Line and the dozen or so people I always seemed to find locked into their perpetual poses whenever I visited, has vanished.

Safety Clowns: I really did drive an ice-cream truck for a day, and that really is all I'm going to say about that day.

Loubob is in name only my friend Lou(Bob), who owns Lou's Records in Encinitas, California. He has never made or animated a muffler man, though he did spend several years failing to rebuild an MG.

Devil's Smile: Like so many of my ideas these days, this one started with my children. More specifically, it emerged while I was reading my kids a book by Donald J. Sobol called *True Sea Adventures* (they're those kinds of kids, fortunately) and discovering the astonishing story of Charles F. Tallman, his boat the *Christina*, and the blizzard of January 7th, 1866. My affection for the wandering chapters of *Moby Dick* generated some of this story too, I'm sure. And my visit to New Bedford, which still feels dark and blubber-soaked and bird-riven and good and strange, even before you stick your head in the Whaling Museum and see the wall of implements for carving up whales at sea—as terrifying and poignant in their shapes as the gynecological instruments for working on "mutant women" in David Cronenberg's *Dead Ringers*—or the photographs of forests of baleen drying on the docks.

Transitway: If you want to know where this story came from, try sitting for five minutes at one of the Harbor Transitway bus stops along the 110 freeway between San Pedro and Los Angeles.

The words "South Central" really have been expunged, by decree of city authorities, from future maps of Los Angeles.

The Muldoon: Book inscription story #2:

Without question, my maternal grandfather rates as one of the most profound influences on my life. Born working-poor in downtown Baltimore, he scratched and worked and worked and scratched his way through law school, shone as a lawyer, became a raging civil rights activist, and wound up an Appellate Court judge, city councilman, and much-loved and controversial Maryland figure. A behemoth in every sense of the word (he weighed well over 300 pounds for most of the years I knew him), he sang leading roles in community theater and starred on the banquet circuit, but he seemed most at home in the sandwich shops near his downtown office or talking to the grinning parking lot crew at Memorial Stadium, all of whom he knew (down to the names of their wives and children). He read passionately, believed relentlessly in working for the public good, had a system for picking horse-track winners that worked, and remained open to an astonishing range of experiences—as long as they didn't involve setting foot outside of Baltimore—for his entire life. His legacy is complicated, joyful, rich, and just plain *large*. He has been dead more than fifteen years, and I still miss him deeply, and think of him in one way or another almost daily.

Mostly, what my grandfather gave me while he was alive, and left me when he died, were books. Primarily, these were his well-read hardbacks with the dustjackets discarded (my grandfather found jackets mostly gaudy and a waste). In many of the books, he left notes for me. Perhaps my favorite, up until just recently, was the one he scrawled in a copy of Lawrence Durrell's *Balthazar*, from *The Alexandria Quartet*. Like many so-serious, writerly late teens, I fell in love with those books, and had been badgering my grandfather for his lovely editions for years, despite his surprising and uncharacteristic resistance. On my 21st birthday, my grandfather finally bestowed this volume upon me. Inside, I found the words:

For Glen. How not *to write.*

Then, last winter, I was snatching books from my shelves to save them from the rain pouring through our crumbling roof when I came across my grandfather's copy of Edwin O'Connor's *The Last Hurrah*. *Good book*, I remember thinking, though it had been decades, literally, since I'd read it. I remembered it had been a favorite of my grandfather's. I opened the front cover and found this:

> For my only literate grand-son. From his Grandfather, who was a Muldoon in his own right.
>
> The Big Judge

The "only literate grand-son" bit proved grossly unfair to and completely inaccurate about both my brother and my cousins. But it was my grandfather's voice, alright, provocative, noisy, opinionated, trying to tell me something. I re-read the whole book that weekend, trying to find what "Muldoon" meant, though I thought I knew. The word barely surfaces in the novel. My friend, the spectacularly gifted poet Darcie Dennigan, asked a list-serve group to which she belongs to do some research, and came back with a scant handful of uses of the term in the press or in public documents over the course of the last century. Most uses, though, circled around the same basic idea: a Muldoon is someone who takes care of his own.

Balcony Ball is a real game, copyright 1973 or so by my brother and me, though it's more than possible my uncle and aunt had a precursor of their own when they lived in that house (my mother had already left for college by the time her family moved there).

Berger cookies may be the best cookies ever to become available in a bag.